PRAISE FOR BARBAR

Gaudí Afternoon

"There hasn't been this much cross-dressing, confusion, and hilarity since Rosalind entered the Forest of Arden." —*Booklist*

"[A] marvelous story of intrigue and shifting identities . . . Language, gender and architecture all deal with the construction of images. In *Gaudí Afternoon*, Wilson weaves them together in a fascinating, multi-layered mystery as labyrinthine as Gaudí's most famous structures."
—*Lambda Book Report*

"*Gaudí Afternoon* is a wickedly hilarious gender-bender."
—*The Toronto Star*

"Wilson's latest mystery [is] a raucous, irreverent story, rich with Barcelonian detail, zany characters and layers of meaning." —*Just Out*

Trouble in Transylvania

"Barbara Wilson's Cassandra Reilly novels, wonderfully witty and fun to read for their stories alone, will be understood and read as classics for centuries to come." —*The Lesbian Review of Books*

"Ms. Wilson's lesbian globe-trotter has a restless nature, a facility for languages and a lively curiosity about foreign cultures. Toss in her offbeat sense of humor and you've got a terrific road pal."
—*New York Times Book Review*

"Murder, revenge, lust, and greed—American family values halfway round the world with a resolution all feminists can sink their teeth into."
—*The Advocate*

ALSO BY BARBARA WILSON

Cassandra Reilly Mysteries:
Gaudí Afternoon
Trouble in Transylvania
The Death of a Much-Travelled Woman

Pam Nilsen Mysteries:
Murder in the Collective
Sisters of the Road
The Dog Collar Murders

Translations from Norwegian:
Cora Sandel: Selected Short Stories
Nothing Happened by Ebba Haslund

Fiction:
If You Had a Family
Cows and Horses
Salt Water and Other Stories

Memoir:
Blue Windows: A Christian Science Childhood

The Case of the Orphaned Bassoonists

A Cassandra Reilly Mystery

BARBARA WILSON

Seal Press

Cover design and art by Clare Conrad
Text design by Alison Rogalsky
Cover photographs by Tere Carranza

Library of Congress Cataloging-in-Publication Data

Wilson, Barbara, 1950–
    The case of the orphaned bassoonists : a Cassandra Reilly mystery / Barbara Wilson.
        p. cm.
    ISBN 1-58005-046-8 (paper)
    1. Reilly, Cassandra (Fictitious character)—Fiction. 2. Women Translators—Fiction. 3. Women musicians—Fiction. 4. Venice (Italy)—Fiction. 5. Lesbians—Fiction. I. Title.

    PS3573.I45678 C37 2000
    813'.54—cd21

                                                                00-044001

Printed in Canada

First printing, October 2000

10   9   8   7   6   5   4   3   2   1

Distributed to the trade by Publishers Group West
In Canada: Publishers Group West Canada, Toronto, Ontario

To James Myhre

Acknowledgments

The letter attributed to Vittoria Brunelli, a fictional character, is taken from a letter by seventeenth-century composer Lavinia della Pietà. It appears in *Women Musicians of Venice*, by Jane L. Baldauf-Berdes (Oxford: Oxford University Press, 1993).

My great thanks to Liana Borghi, Tere Carranza, Faith Conlon, Cathy Johnson, Gail and Betsy Leondar-Wright, Cristina Manozzi and Pat Mullan.

The transcendent music is that of the asylums. There are four of them, made up of illegitimate and orphaned girls whose parents are not in a position to raise them. They are brought up at the expense of the state and trained solely to excel in music. Moreover, they sing like angels and play the violin, the flute, the organ, the oboe, the cello and the bassoon; in short, there is no instrument, however unwieldy, that can frighten them. They are cloistered like nuns. It is they alone who perform, and about forty girls take part in each concert. I vow to you that there is nothing so diverting as the sight of a young and pretty nun in white habit, with a bunch of pomegranate blossoms over her ear, conducting the orchestra and beating time with all the grace and precision imaginable.

—Charles de Brosses
an eighteenth-century visitor to Venice

The Case of the Orphaned Bassoonists

One

It BEGAN SIMPLY, a malicious prank or a robbery pinned on the wrong person, nothing to take too seriously.

It began with the disappearance of a musical instrument.

"But why would you even want another bassoon, Nicky? You already have four."

My friend Nicola Gibbons was calling me from Venice. She'd left London just four days ago to attend a symposium on women musicians of Vivaldi's time. If she'd had a lesser voice, I would have hardly been able to hear her. For it was an evening in late October and a violent wind knocked tree limbs against the house and sent dust bin lids spinning. A thin rain spat and spewed.

"Of course I didn't *take* the bloody bassoon, Cassandra, but the fact is, it's gone missing while supposedly in my possession, and it's a period piece, priceless and irreplaceable, and I'm apparently responsible."

I repressed a sigh. Why was she calling *me*? I couldn't exactly tell her that she was interrupting a very pleasant evening, one that I very much deserved after the trip I'd just made. Since I travel constantly and keep my attic room at Nicky's house in London only as a base, I had been thrilled to find myself arriving as she was leaving, and to discover that I was quite alone in her house, with the prospect of a week to enjoy her good wines, her library and her specially made large bathtub.

"But they're not planning to put you in jail or anything, are they?" I interrupted her, hoping she would come to the point.

"No, I'm not really even under arrest. But the police have searched my room several times and questioned me pretty thoroughly and now they're telling me I can't leave the country, or else I really will be arrested. They took my passport."

I had the electric fire on and a small whisky on the coffee table. I took a sip, and then another as Nicky ranted on, and flipped through a magazine on my lap. Beside me on the sofa sat a pile of books in Spanish. I was supposed to review them for an editor at a large London publishing house. I'd picked them up from Simon earlier today.

"Most of them are just literary novels," Simon had sighed. "But here's one that looks promising. It's by a protégé of Gloria de los Angeles. It was described to me at the Frankfurt Book Fair as 'the erotic and spiritual struggles of a group of eighteenth-century Venezuelan nuns.'"

I'd put *Lovers and Virgins* on top of the pile, along with a book called *Bashō in Lima,* which seemed to be about a woman of Japanese-Peruvian descent making a pilgrimage back to Peru. The other novels had less riveting covers, and one, at least, was about Latin American politics. "I hate to be an unfeeling Philistine," Simon had said, "but these books about military coups and disappeared people don't sell anymore. Sexy nuns, well, that's another story. Let me have your reports in a couple of weeks, darling."

It felt good to be back to some sort of work, and good to be back in London. I had just returned from an unfortunate excursion to several of the more distant tropical islands with a naturalist who was studying turtle migration. Although charming, Angela had been rather more scientific than amorous and while I had learned a great deal about turtles, I'd also badly bruised my hip after stumbling over some rocks along the shore. Not only had the fall put me out of temper, it had also caused me to crush some extremely rare turtle eggs, putting Angela out of temper with me as well.

I was looking forward to a quiet autumn, nursing my still-painful hip and sniffing around for something reasonably lucrative to translate. Although *Bashō in Lima* tantalized, I put it aside for the heftier novel. Translation paid by the word, which was unfortunate when a book seemed to be full of haiku and white space.

"Shall I call your solicitor?" I interrupted Nicky finally, when she showed signs of coming to the end of excoriating the Italian police and judicial system.

"For the moment I'd prefer to handle this myself. At least until I can sort out the real story and see what my responsibility . . ." Her normally booming voice dropped to a whisper. It seemed someone had come into her room.

"Responsibility? But you said you didn't . . ."

"No, I didn't take the fiendish *fagotto!*" Her words seemed to be directed to whoever was in the room.

"Really, Nicky," I worried. "Do you think you should be talking to them like that?"

"*Fagotto* is bassoon, Cassandra." Her voice was now impatient. Her visitor had apparently gone out again. Nicky often had that effect on people. "I need you to come to Venice, and I especially need you to bring some books and papers from my study. I'll tell you which ones." She began to rattle off a list as I searched for my pen. I scribbled the items on the cover of *Lovers and Virgins*. Nicky made me read them back to her: a biography, a music program, some copies of articles and interviews, which I'd find in a file cabinet. Additionally I was to find and bring an envelope marked PRIVATE and a largish sum of money from a safe hidden in the study. I would find the combination in a jar of lentils in the kitchen.

"But can't I just send all this? It would be one thing if you were in jail, Nicky. But you know I've just come back from a long trip, and I have to read a whole stack of Latin American books for Simon."

"I *am* practically in jail. With *her* watching me all the time. Even professional jealousy is preferable to this kind," she hissed.

"But . . ."

"For god's sakes, lass," Nicky shouted, her Glaswegian accent suddenly strong, "Can't you understand that I *need* you?"

As always, Nicky as a Scottish warrior queen suddenly down on her luck was irresistible.

"I'll be there tomorrow," I said.

I always liked going into Nicky's study, but I rarely visited it without her present. Although she wouldn't have minded, my reticence was a holdover from the days when it had been Olivia Wulf's study. By the time I met Olivia, she seemed several hundred years old to me, as clever as a snake and as refined as a string of pearls. Her cultured air intimidated me. Nicky had grown up in an intellectual if impoverished family; the only person in my family who had read a book was my Aunt Eavan in Chicago. No one was artistic, and no one played music, though my father did sing, and in a lovely tenor, too, when he was in his cups.

The study's walls were nearly covered with bookshelves, but here and there hung framed sketches and photographs of both Olivia and Nicky. Tall, with her smooth blond hair pulled back in a low knot, in strapless gowns and pearls, Olivia looked polished and stunning. Nicky, on the other hand, never looked polished. What I'd always liked about Nicky was her lack of proportion and sedateness. It wasn't just her size; it was her moon face, her big hands and feet, the curls that shot out in auburn corkscrews from her head. She was never afraid to look ugly, and she did look ugly, quite often. But then again, she could look gorgeous, and these performance photographs (bassoon in hand) showed it. Hair swept up, shoulders bare, cleavage deep and compelling. She had a propensity for hats, capes and tall boots, for velvet and satin, for colors like maroon and violet and rose-mauve. Her eyelashes were long, and her voice, when not rattling the windows, was rich with possibility. She had never been short of admirers, male and female.

In her youth Olivia had been beautiful, and she too had had many lovers, along with an apparently long-suffering husband who was a musician as well. He'd been arrested in 1937 while on tour in Berlin and had had a heart attack while being "questioned." Nicky had told me that one of Olivia's old flames managed to get her out of Vienna and to London. Her twenty-year-old son, Jakob, was supposed to come with her, but at the last minute he'd disappeared. Olivia always thought it was because he hadn't wanted to leave his fiancée, Elizabeth, who wasn't Jewish. He died at Dachau in 1940 from pneumonia. Olivia had never been able to find out what happened to Elizabeth. Nicky became the grandchild she'd never had.

The photographs showed that Olivia had successfully made a new life for herself as a teacher and member of the London Symphony Orchestra. But that life was drawing to a close when I came to stay in the attic room. In her last years she seemed only old and forgetful, needing Nicky's constant attention.

Six months ago Olivia died and left everything to Nicky.

The phone rang again while I was staring at the photographs. When I picked up the receiver, a woman's voice said, in a British accent that was good but hardly perfect, "Your friend Nicola asked me to call." She did not identify herself. The wind outside made it difficult to hear her clearly.

"Is anything wrong?"

"Sorry, sorry. No reason for alarm. It's only that she feels perhaps she was hasty. Now everything is solved, there's no need to come."

"Oh, I see," I said. "Is Nicky there?"

"No, she's packing to return to England. Everything is fine." Her vehemence was unmistakably false, and I didn't believe a word she'd said.

"Well, that's good news," I said. "Good-bye."

I put the phone down and continued collecting the things Nicky had asked for.

Some were easy. The biography of a well-known and now dead conductor was right on the shelf where it should have been, and, stuffed in a box with other programs, was one from an international Vivaldi festival that had taken place in Venice a few years ago, on the 250th anniversary of Vivaldi's death. But the copies of articles Nicky wanted were harder to locate. Though Nicky had a filing system that worked for her, my own mind was organized differently, and I looked for something to do with bassoons before coming across a cache of articles in a hanging file labeled "Orphanages of Venice." The hanging file was the right one, and I pulled from it a manila folder labeled "Musicians of the Pietà."

Most of the articles were by an Andrew McManus, who lived in Winnipeg, but a few were in Swedish and German. There was also a waggishly titled interview with Nicky herself from a British music journal: "The Case of the Orphaned Bassoonists." In the accompanying photo, Nicky was holding a Venetian mask, as well as a period

8

bassoon, and looking a bit coy.

Nicky, when asked, always said she chose to play the bassoon because it was so large. Nobody messed her about after school when she was carrying an instrument whose hard case doubled as a weapon. But to me, the bassoon seemed to suit her because it was more a speaking instrument than a singing one. It didn't trill or soar like the flute or clarinet; it ruminated, low-pitched and sometimes argumentative; it bubbled with ideas, it sighed and laughed. Other instruments might cry; the bassoon wept quietly, even glumly. More often it just discussed the whole question thoroughly.

Standing in the study, I skimmed one of the articles by Andrew McManus. It was a pity his prose was so dull, for the ideas were quite interesting. Venice had had a long tradition of opening *ospedali*—charitable institutions for the sick and destitute—for abandoned and orphaned children. One of Venice's *ospedali*, the Pietà, specialized in foundlings and, particularly, teaching musically talented girl foundlings to sing in the many liturgical rites required in the Venetian churches. Beginning in the 1600s, all the *ospedali* made a point of musical education and performance, and by the early 1700s they were running musical conservatories that parented girls in the city vied to attend.

The girls sang everything from soprano to bass and played every instrument in orchestras that were famous all over Europe. Over three hundred teachers, mostly male, were employed by the *ospedali*, as well as composers and choirmasters. The priest Antonio Vivaldi was perhaps the most famous of the Ospedale della Pietà's choirmasters. He began as a violin teacher at the Pietà in 1703, and later served as Master of Concerts at that institution for most of the rest of his life, composing hundreds of musical pieces for the all-female orchestra of the Pietà.

I turned to the interview with Nicola:

9

Interviewer: It should be no surprise that Vivaldi, who was a brilliant violinist, composed so many pieces for the violin.

Nicola Gibbons: It's no surprise at all. There are several hundred sonatas and concertos for the violin—solo, double, with *basso continuo* and orchestra. Hundreds. By all accounts Vivaldi must have trained young violinists by the dozen at the Pietà. So the really curious thing is that he also composed thirty-nine concertos for the bassoon.

Interviewer: That's an unusually high number.

NG: Speaking as one who knows the bassoon repertoire, it's an incredibly high number. Especially since his players were all women, and they don't tend to be associated with the bassoon.

Interviewer: He obviously was drawn to something about the bassoon . . . And, yet, you're right, it's curious. Women have been more traditionally linked with the piano, the harp, the flute.

NG: Exactly! It makes you wonder whether he had one or more very stunning bassoonists whom he was working with at the Pietà. I would love to know.

Interviewer: Let's talk about the media project you're hoping to get off the ground. You've said it's a recording of up to six CDs, Vivaldi's complete bassoon concertos on CD-ROM, as performed by an all women's orchestra in period dress, using period instruments. Do you worry that it might be a bit repetitive? Some people say that Vivaldi wrote the same concerto four hundred times.

NG: I don't agree. I think the bassoon concertos would make a terrific CD-ROM program! It would be great fun to dramatize the whole thing.

Interviewer (laughs): Who would you get to play Vivaldi?

NG (laughs): Oh, Ralph Fiennes, I think. Is he at all musical?

I shook my head. Surely it was a harmless enough obsession of

Nicky's, this search for legitimate bassoon-playing foremothers. It kept her out of the kind of trouble her mother had always prophesied she'd land in. Until now, anyway.

I went into the kitchen to poke around in the lentils for the combination to the safe, and then returned to the study. I was shocked at the amount of money inside the safe. Wasn't that why banks were invented? I was also shocked at the amount Nicky expected me to bring to her. It was one thing to say it aloud on the phone; it was another to count it out in bills and stuff it in a small paper bag. How could she possibly need this much money?

The answer might lie in the envelope marked PRIVATE, but it was firmly sealed with tape. I shook the envelope but all that seemed to be in it was paper. I put everything I'd collected into a small bag and began to turn out the lamps in the study. I was reluctant to think too much more about all this tonight. Surely Nicky would explain everything when I saw her.

When the lights were all off but one, I stopped and put on an old cassette tape of Nicky and Olivia playing a Vivaldi piece. I sat down on the couch, no longer an interloper, remembering all the years when I, the avowedly nonmusical one, would perch on the attic stairs and listen to the bassoon and violin singing together below.

Two

ONCE BEFORE I'D FLOWN into Venice, on a spring morning spun of blue sky and water. I'd looked down to see the islands flung across the lagoon, had seen Venice itself through a light wash of clouds, and it had seemed to me like an ancient map, with fading blue and ochre inks charting the outlines of sea and shore. The swirl of the Grand Canal had slipped through the city like the fanciful S of an illuminated manuscript.

But this time, a humid twilight was falling and I could see little as the plane descended into Marco Polo Airport. I'd meant to read through the articles from Nicky's files on the flight. I'd also meant to give a serious look at *Bashō in Lima* and a couple of the other books I'd brought with me, if only to get them firmly out of the way and off the list. Instead I'd become thoroughly engrossed in the first chapters of *Lovers and Virgins*. I could see I was going to have trouble resisting its headlong plot. The characters might be pasteboard, the dialogue stiff and romantic, and the narrative as ridiculous as anything that the author's mentor Gloria de los Angeles, the queen of magic realism, had ever devised. All the same, I was hooked. What would happen to the four girls in the Venezuelan colonial family? I'd had hints from the reviews. Lourdes saw visions. Mercedes loved books. Maria would be deflowered by a handsome stable boy, and Isabella was her mother's right hand. Which of the sisters would become nuns and which lovers? Like many ex-Catholics, I had never lost my secret fascination with nuns and what they really did under those voluminous robes.

I took the airport bus to the Piazzale Roma and then a *vaporetto* down the Grand Canal. There is always a sense of magic and disorientation when arriving in Venice. Your mind panics a little, tells you, *Flooded. The streets are flooded.* But your imagination, so much closer to the dreaming state, murmurs, *Yes, and isn't this how life should be? Simply stepping onto boats instead of buses or cars, gliding easily between tiny ports of call?* Tonight Venice was wet and trembling. Explosions of thunder came from all directions—sometimes far away, sometimes right overhead, as if the city were being demolished. I half expected, when lightning scoured the face of an ancient *palazzo*, that the thunder following would break it to dust and rubble.

I stepped off the *vaporetto* at the Accademia stop, in the Dorsoduro district, just as it began to pour. My sore hip slowed me down, but, pulling my luggage behind me like a rectangular dog, I began to make my way through the streaming little streets to the address Nicky had given me. It had been a long while since I'd been in Venice, and, in any case, it's not the kind of city whose map is easy to recall from one visit to the next. The spring I'd been here, I'd been content to wander without paying attention to my itinerary.

Within minutes I was lost, of course. Narrow passages opened into empty squares with a dozen exits. Canals forced streets to dead-end, and bridges multiplied with bewildering complexity. I hadn't remembered to bring an umbrella (I was going south, after all) and was soon soaked. The wind carried the salty smell of the Adriatic.

It wasn't until I'd crossed the width of the Dorsoduro and come out on the Záttere, the promenade that faces the island of Giudecca, that I could see where I was. I read the map again, asked for directions at a café, and plunged back into the maze of streets. In the strange way of things, I found the address easily this time, perhaps because I halted awkwardly when I saw a pair of lovers taking shelter in a doorway, and in my confusion looked away from them and saw the number Nicky had given me on a large house across the canal.

The *palazzo* was in a garden full of dripping trees and rain-darkened statues. Up a few marble steps was a huge door with peeling paint and a knocker in the shape of a lion's head. I knocked and heard footsteps echoing off a tile floor in the manner of a gothic novel. I expected an aging manservant in threadbare golden livery to open the door, but it was Nicky.

"Good! You're finally here," she said, not bothering to give me more than a cursory kiss on the cheek. "I've been through hell."

She didn't look it. Or rather, she looked as if hell agreed with her. Even though I'd known Nicky for twenty years, the forcefulness of her appearance could still surprise me, especially if I ran into her anywhere outside her house in Hampstead. Her London residence contained her, accommodated her. When you saw her at home in the kitchen wearing her lipstick-red satin dressing gown, you didn't think, *What a gigantic force of nature the woman is*. You merely thought, *Here's Nicky having her morning cuppa*.

Now she seemed to fill the doorway in a long maroon tunic reminiscent of the latter days of the Roman Empire, though a shawl around her shoulders and reading glasses pushed up into her spiraling auburn curls lent a more domestic look. As usual she was wearing expensive and somewhat complicated shoes; Nicky was proud of her well-shaped ankles.

14

"Come upstairs," she said, leading the way up marble stairs to a bedroom with enormous ceilings and dusty gold drapes. A chandelier poured from above. The double bed was covered with Nicky's clothes, and shoes were flung every which way over the flowered carpet, as if she'd been throwing them at ghosts. On the wall was a large gilt-framed School of Tiepolo painting that showed the Virgin Mary being sucked into a vortex of angels.

"Did you bring what I asked you to? Thank you, by the way."

I handed over the bag and then perched on the edge of the bed. "A thousand pounds is a lot of money," I ventured.

Nicky only snorted. "This whole situation is extremely annoying, to say the least. I have a concert in Birmingham tomorrow. Quite a number of people are going to be furious if I'm not there. I have no idea how long these Italians think they can keep me in Venice."

"Why don't you tell me what happened?"

"I got here five days ago for the symposium. There are about fifteen of us, I suppose, a combination of scholars and musicians. Some of us were put up in this house, which belongs to the man who organized the event, Alfredo Sandretti. I've hardly seen him by the way, except when it's time to give a flowery speech; he makes his son do all the work.

"Anyway here we are." Nicky paced around the room, counting off: "Me, Gunther from Germany, Andrew from Canada and Bitten from Sweden. All of us have performed Vivaldi's bassoon concertos. Bitten Johansson is probably Scandinavia's best-known Baroque bassoonist. Andrew isn't the most brilliant player, but he's made himself an expert on Vivaldi. I didn't realize he'd begun to focus exclusively on the Pietà. He's a professor and is just starting a sabbatical to write a book about his research here. Anyway, I suppose they put us together because they thought we'd have a lot to talk about. There's an oboist staying here too, Dutch or something, probably because they didn't have anywhere else to stash her."

Nicky ran her hands through her curls, newly colored and full of life. My own hair was curly too, but frizzier and getting gray. I usually tucked it into a beret and forgot about it.

"The idea was that we would participate in seminars during the day and in the evening play music. Each day we were loaned period instruments to practice on. Then, after practicing, they'd take the instruments away again and give them back to us at the concert. Yesterday, the last day of the symposium, everything was a little more lax; we had a long lunch and then only a bit of a late rehearsal. Everyone was tired, to tell the truth. We kept the instruments with us, as it was only a few hours until the performance. I took a nap, fell deeply asleep, and when I woke up, the bassoon I'd been lent was gone.

"There was an enormous search—Sandretti, his son, the police, everybody sniffing through my knickers. I couldn't imagine they were serious. I couldn't *believe* anyone thought I'd taken it. And *why* would I do it before the last concert, when it would be so obvious?"

"Is it worth a lot?"

"Of course, though it could have been worse. It's not a classic, like a Denner or Hotteterre. But it *is* one of the instruments once used by the Pietà girls. Belongs to the Sandrettis, in the family for centuries. I don't know the price, or even if there is one. In Italy everything is millions of *lire* anyway. But how do you value something that is one of a kind?"

She stuck the money and the envelope marked PRIVATE between the mattresses without further explanation. Then she picked up the biography of the conductor and began flipping impatiently through it. I pulled off my boots. They made a sorry impression next to Nicky's red heels. She'd tried for years to make me more fashion-conscious, but I'd stuck to my black Levi's and boots. It was one of

16

my few consistencies.

A knock at the door interrupted Nicky's reading, and a beautiful young man entered with a tray. Ah, the faithful retainer at last and none too soon, for I was hungry, and the sight of biscuits and cheese with a carafe of wine was particularly welcome.

"Marco Sandretti. Cassandra Reilly," Nicky said in a clipped, even hostile manner. Since Nicky usually enjoyed the company of attractive young people, I could only surmise that she considered him to be if not an enemy, then of the enemy camp. "Why does everyone else get to go out and I have to stay here?"

"I'm very sorry," said Marco. "My father told me for you to stay here."

"Your father, your father!" said Nicky, pacing and eating biscuits. She looked like Maria Callas as Medea in her heavy days. "I never should have accepted his invitation to come to this symposium. Oh yes, he made it sound so lovely. A week in sunny Italy with gorgeous meals and the enchanting company of like-minded musicians. Ha!"

"We will go out tonight for a very nice meal," said Marco, looking hunted. "And your friends, they don't go far. It is raining. I am sorry," he added again.

There was another knock on the door, and a man in his late thirties came in. He went purposefully up to Marco as if to claim an embrace, but the Italian adroitly sidestepped him.

"You have not yet met Nicola's friend. Cassandra Reilly. Andrew McManus."

Andrew was good-looking, but not in the dark, questioning, romantic way of Marco. Andrew was more on the order of a well-designed cereal box. His head sat thickly on his shoulders, which were narrow but powerful. His waist was low and his upper torso pumped up by big, strong lungs. His legs, on the other hand, were short and spindly, ending in heavy shoes, as if to balance him.

In spite of the flatness of his features, his face was oddly colorful. The freckled skin had an orangish cast, the eyes were blue, the mouth very red. When he smiled at me, he looked more dutiful than charmed. He made another awkward leap at Marco, which was again quickly foiled.

In a minute, two more people entered the room. I realized they were the couple I'd seen clandestinely embracing outside.

"Bitten and Gunther," Nicky said with no great enthusiasm.

"Hello," said the pair with an equal lack of interest in me. It was taking all their energy to keep their hands off each other. I managed a hello as well, though I was gaping impolitely at Bitten Johansson.

She was almost six feet tall, a stunningly beautiful older woman dressed in a coral silk shirt and cool gray-blond linen pants suit with a hip-length jacket. Her hair, the same color as the linen suit, was thick and parted on the side, and she wasn't wearing much makeup, only eyeliner, which elongated her frosty blue eyes. The only thing that seemed remotely untidy about this striking woman was that three, that is to say all but one, of the buttons on her silk blouse were undone, and she was wearing no bra. Was it Swedish lack of inhibition? Or were her bassoonist's lungs so powerful that they had split the blouse open?

Gunther was also a strapping blond specimen with delicate but strong lips, a firm jaw line, a wide chest and a half-zipped fly. He looked to be in his thirties, a good fifteen years younger than Bitten.

Should their dishabille be pointed out? The tinny, insistent ring of a cell phone sounded in the awkward silence.

"Please," said Gunther. "I must speak to my Handy." He turned slightly away. "Ja, ja, Frigga," we heard him saying. Was his Handy his cell phone or his wife?

Bitten approached me. "So, you came to help your friend?" she said blandly, with some secret threat attached to the word *help*.

"If I can." Was this the *she* Nicky had railed against in her phone call? More important was this the *she* who had called to dissuade me from coming to Venice? The admiration I'd first experienced for Bitten's gorgeous physique turned quickly to dislike as she glared at me. No, it didn't look as though we would become pals.

Nicky interrupted. "Bitten your shirt, Button. I mean, button it, Bitten, for pity's sake. You look like a tart." I noticed Nicky had done something with the book she'd been flipping through. The maroon tunic, perhaps, had absorbed it, like some great fish swallowing a minnow.

Slowly Bitten took her Arctic blue eyes off me and looked down. "Oh my goodness," she said vaguely and glanced over at Gunther, who was still saying, "*Ja, ja*, Frigga."

Marco said, "In only a few minutes we are going for dinner to a place very close to here."

"I suppose you've heard," Andrew said, finally addressing me, "that although Nicky is the one they suspect, they're making all four of us continue to stay on here."

"But you don't suspect her, do you?" I asked him. "I mean, really."

"Of course not," he said, but his eyes shifted just a little.

Bitten said, "Well, the fact is, the bassoon is still missing. If it would come back, then our problems would be solved. We could all leave." There was no mistaking the hateful look she gave Nicky.

"Then why don't you return it?" snapped Nicky.

"I object. I object. You had the bassoon, the room was locked, how could I possibly take it? And anyway, I feel that we had a sacred trust with these instruments. They represent the soul of the *cori*."

"Oh, stuff it," said Nicky.

Gunther got off his cell phone with a final cheerful but impatient,

"*Ja*, Frigga."

The caller must have been his wife, because Bitten was giving him the cold shoulder. He looked at her pleadingly and then noticed he was unzipped, which made him blush.

"Well," said Marco brightly. "Is everyone ready for dinner? We will go to the same nice place," he said. "Squid in its own ink, its specialty, you remember."

"Oh, delightful," said Bitten. "Squid in its own ink, definitely the sort of thing you can eat night after night. Why should we be punished just because *she* . . ."

Andrew said, "I think we should respect the task Marco has taken on. It's no easy matter for him to keep us together and amused." Disgusted grunts around him showed that *amused* was slightly the wrong choice.

Marco looked around. "Are we all . . .?"

It was then I noticed that someone else had slipped into the room, a middle-aged, nondescript woman with short brown hair, wearing a brown raincoat. The Dutch oboist perhaps?

"Miss de Hoog," said Marco. "Cassandra Reilly."

We shook hands briefly. She had clever eyes that did not quite fit the studied politeness of her expression.

Outside, I fell into step with Marco, forcing Andrew to walk ahead with Nicky. Gunther and Bitten walked side by side, without speaking, behind us, and Miss de Hoog brought up the rear. The rain had stopped, but the clouds still whipped about. The canal beside the house slopped over into the street. Everything was wet and shiny.

"Your friend Nicola," said Marco cautiously, "she is a very large, I mean big-hearted woman. But she don't like me."

"I'm sure you realize, Marco, that she's in a bit of a difficult position here. Nobody likes to be suspected of stealing a bassoon."

"Oh, it's all very complicated," he sighed. "My father is very sad to go to the police. He has much admiration for your friend and her playing. And also for the great interest she shows in the girls."

Was that the true problem here? "Which girls?" I asked cautiously.

"Girls from long ago. The *cori* of the *ospedali*. It is a long tradition here in Venice. Very remarkable. Your friend, *she* is remarkable."

"Yes, she is, and as her long-time friend, I have to say you're barking up the wrong tree. Nicky would never steal anything valuable." I put out of my mind the time she'd pinched a lover of mine. "When the true culprit comes to light, you can bet it won't be Nicky." (But why did she need all that money? Was she being blackmailed? Had she hired someone else to steal the bassoon for her?)

Looking at Nicky's substantial back and powerful stride, Marco could not help sighing. "I am still hoping that all this can be resoluted illegally," he said, rather hopelessly.

Three

MISS DE HOOG'S SKIN was not really chalk gray—it was not that un-healthy—but it had a dusty cast to it that would have flattened even more memorable features. Her mouth was pale, her nose nothing special, and her eyes were as gray as a metal strongbox and just as impenetrable. She would never be the first person noticed in a group. She would not be the one you remembered afterwards. In a photo-graph taken of an event where she was present, it was likely she would be half-concealed behind someone else or have her eyes closed against the sun. She was so unremarkable that you wouldn't expect anyone to point to the picture and ask, "And who was that?"

And yet her body was solid and strong. I noticed, when she en-tered the restaurant in front of me and took off her raincoat, that her shoulders were broad and that her calves, under the slightly too-long skirt, looked muscled, as if she were a cyclist. Certainly her fin-gers had tensile strength; I'd felt that when we shook hands earlier.

For a fleeting moment, as I seated myself next to her, I thought, *She's disguising herself as an ugly woman.* But that was no doubt only whimsy. The fact is, over the years I had met many musicians, and Nicky's dramatic appearance was the exception. Most orchestra players were ordinary looking, even drab: vessels or reeds through which the sublimity of Mozart or Sibelius poured.

To my first questions, Miss de Hoog, or Anna as she now allowed her first name to be, was respectfully indifferent. About her nationality and residence, she answered politely that she was Belgian and had been born in Antwerp, but that her work took her to second-string cities everywhere. "I am a rather minor oboist," she said with unfeigned modesty. "But I always have appointments."

She discouraged further attempts to pin her down. Since I often do the same—and, in fact, did do the same when Anna de Hoog tried to pin *me* down—I couldn't blame her. "No, I don't live much of anywhere either, I'm afraid. I'm usually traveling," I said.

"And your travels are for pleasure or for . . ."

"Pleasure mostly." Not an untruth, but I found myself reluctant to indulge her curiosity when she eluded mine. Still, I persisted in trying to draw her out. For Nicky sat in funereal splendor, eating her starter and then pasta with (for her) little appetite, and ignoring Marco, who tried to talk with her, though Andrew had him pretty well monopolized with cunning questions about Italian soccer teams. Gunther and Bitten were preoccupied with each other, talking in low tones in German or staring semicovertly at each other's body parts. Seen side by side the two of them did make a handsome, if overly tall, pair. They reminded me of a children's book I'd read long ago, about a Mr. Giant who is lonely until he finds a Miss Giant to share his life.

It was only when we began to talk about the Venetian *ospedali* that Anna de Hoog grew animated.

"It's a very recent passion of mine," she said. "Of course I've always played Vivaldi. But I had little idea that so many of his

23

compositions were written for girls. I find that very charming. Very inspiring. The symposium really opened my eyes to the rich legacy of these *cori*. Do you realize there were hundreds of women musicians whose names we are just beginning to discover? Who knows what treasures are hidden in archives and private libraries?" For a second Anna's shadowy face looked quite transformed. "In another life, how I would love to spend my life playing the oboe."

Gunther hadn't said anything till now. Laughing, he said to Anna, "But you *do* play the oboe. You mean, you'd love to spend your life playing the work of the women musicians!"

"Well, now there's one less treasure in the Sandretti library," Andrew put in. In spite of his knowledge of soccer, he seemed to be getting nowhere with Marco.

"We must not be quick to judgment," Anna de Hoog murmured.

"What is the story behind the bassoon that was taken?" I asked, taking advantage of my innocent status as a stranger.

"Why don't *you* tell her, Andrew?" said Nicky sullenly. "Since you're the expert."

I had the strong sense that Nicky, with her long and well-established interest in the women bassoonists, could not have been too pleased to arrive in Venice and find Andrew getting ready to write a book on the subject. She was a little touchy about academics in general, being a self-taught scholar herself.

"So far I only know what Marco's father has told me," said Andrew. "When I come to write my book about the Pietà, I'll of course understand much more. But what is interesting about this particular bassoon is that it survived two hundred years in the Sandretti family."

"The Brunelli family," Marco put in. "My mother's family."

"No bassoons from the Pietà are known to exist, except this one. The Correr Museum, I believe, has the largest collection of instruments from the *ospedali*, mostly violins and cellos, horns, even a pianoforte, but this is—was—the only bassoon."

"What were the rest of you playing on?" I asked.

"For the most part, reproductions," Gunther explained. "They call them period instruments, but often they are re-creations. That's especially true with the bassoon. With the violin, it's different. You cannot make an imitation Stradivarius, but an old bassoon and a new bassoon made to look like an old one—well, they sound quite the same."

"Oh, Gunther, no," said Bitten. "The soul of old bassoons is different." Their eyes locked again, and they clutched each other under the table, as the waiters appeared with our dishes.

"Ah," said Marco to me, "Here is your *fegato*, a specialty of Venice."

"*Fagotto*? Funny, it doesn't look like a bassoon."

"No, no, *fegato* is . . ."

"Liver," said Andrew, with a touch of lasciviousness.

It was the only touch of humor in an otherwise gloomy gathering.

I had assumed I'd be staying in the villa with my friend the suspected bassoon thief, but when we emerged from the restaurant, Marco told me otherwise. The palazzo's rooms were all spoken for. I would be more comfortable in a hotel, and he had taken the liberty of booking me a room.

"It is the hotel where Ruskin wrote *The Rocks of Venezia*," he said enthusiastically and then paused. "Perhaps it is *Stones*? Yes."

I bid good-night to everyone at the *palazzo* and, again pulling my suitcase behind me, set off for the nearby hotel. As we parted Nicky had whispered, "I'll explain soon." Why couldn't she tell me now? What was she waiting for? Whom was she afraid of?

At the hotel, the clerk asked for my passport. I always travel with two—an American one and an Irish—and out of habit I use the Irish, since that generally keeps prices down and earns me more sympathy. But for the moment I could find only the American one, which I presented, and then I went upstairs and fell into a deep but muddled sleep.

When I woke in the morning, I went to the window and opened the shutters. I looked down on the wide stone seaside promenade of the Záttere and across to the island of Giudecca, whose churches wore cowls of white mist. The tide was high. I could see that the waters had risen over the embankment and spilled onto the pavement below.

I could have had breakfast in the hotel, but decided to celebrate my first real day in Venice by going over to the Piazza San Marco for coffee. I put on half my wardrobe to ward off the morning chill and took *Lovers and Virgins* with me. In spite of myself, I could already feel its seductive rhythm invading my brain. Taking the short *vaporetto* ride from Accademia to San Marco, I found myself thinking, *The ancient city rose from the sea like a cache of pastel seashells wrapped in tissue. As Cassandra caught her first glimpse of the Palace of the Doges, she clasped her hands tightly. "My destiny awaits me here!" she murmured.*

The unnamed woman narrator of *Bashō in Venice* would be more likely to murmur:

Through the mist
Ancient pillar
An old lion
Yawns.

The reality was damper and saltier. Wooden platforms had been placed like boardwalks over the paving stones now covered by the high tide. When I reached the grand *piazza*, I found it flooded with an inch or so of the Adriatic; at the same time, fog seemed to pour down into the enormous square. It was like being in the midst of a giant scientific experiment, with liquid at the bottom of the beaker and clouds of condensation rising, falling and swirling all around me.

It was early, and only the most die-hard tourists were about; most people were on their way to work. The cafés were open, but only a single person sat among the dozens of rows of outdoor tables. Through the rising and falling mist the man made a peculiar figure in the *piazza*. He was slender and dressed all in black: black trench coat, black shirt tightly buttoned at his neck, black galoshes and a black bowler hat. The hat was familiar and so were the black leather gloves, which I knew were as thin as latex.

As I drew closer, I saw that he was reading Ruskin's *Stones of Venice*, and it wasn't the abridged version.

"Albert?" I said, still unbelieving, tip-toeing through the water to get to his table. "Albert!"

Albert Egmont, known as "the Egg" because of his bald head, and I had met under competitive circumstances once in Norway, both of us searching for a painter called Cecilia Alcarón. I recalled, with a slight frisson of pleasure, how I had eventually discovered Cecilia's identity and managed to send Albert packing on a boat in a fjord in the middle of nowhere.

Not that either of us would acknowledge remembering the exact details.

"Cassandra Reilly," I pretended to remind him. "Romance translator."

He gave his mysterious, surprisingly sweet smile. "Cassandra, my dear." He lifted his black bowler hat. Beneath it he was perfectly pink and smooth. "What on earth brings you to Venice?"

"A brief holiday," I said. "Change of scene." I sat down and put my feet up on another chair to keep them from getting soaked.

"Well, it is a change from England, isn't it?" he said in his strong Manchester accent. Albert had an art and antique shop in Buxton, a former spa town in the Peak District. "Though I'm not sure I would have seen you as a Venetian type. You seem more Florentine: sunnier, earthier somehow. The Venetians have always been elaborate, recondite, convoluted. Or as Ruskin says, *Gothic*. You know, Ruskin found the Renaissance terribly tedious. Hated the Florentines."

There was an insult somewhere in there, but it still made me laugh. "Are you here on business?"

"One might say business, dear one. I prefer to call it a bit of a look around. A chat here and there. Perhaps something will turn up." But he winked. "And, as Henry James said, 'Almost everyone interesting, appealing, melancholy, memorable, odd, seems at one time or another, after many days and much life, to have gravitated to Venice.'"

The waiter approached with a cappuccino, and Albert spoke to him in respectable Italian. He ordered a cappuccino for me too. Clearly I needed to put my pleasure in triumphing over Albert in the matter of Cecilia behind me, and recognize that, at the moment, the Egg might be quite a useful person with whom to reacquaint myself.

"I don't suppose you know anything about wind instruments, do you?" I asked, after a moment.

"Clarinets, oboes and so on?"

"Bassoons, actually."

"Ah, yes, bassoons." He eyed me speculatively. "Have you lost one, found one or taken one up in a dramatic career change?"

"Lost one, actually. That is, a friend of mine had a very expensive Baroque bassoon loaned to her, and she, ah, seems to have misplaced it."

Albert raised the foamy cup of coffee to his lips with his black-gloved fingers. "Not easy to misplace a bassoon. Of course," he added, "anything can go missing—if someone else takes a fancy to it."

Albert thought a moment. "I have a few acquaintances in the same trade here," he finally said. "Respectable, of course, but they keep their eyes open. As you probably know, beautiful old things in Italy get misplaced with distressing frequency."

"Perfect," I said, though I felt a little uneasy. Was it wise to mix Nicola up with Albert's "respectable" friends? I kept thinking of that huge pile of bank notes I'd brought over for her. There was more to this story than I knew. Still, I gave Albert the details, as best as I could.

"Paper?" he asked. "Pen?" I pulled out a pen and my notebook. In my haste, *Lovers and Virgins* spilled out too, into the inch of water that still swirled under us.

Albert retrieved the book. On the cover was the scribbled list of things Nicola had asked me to bring to Venice. Something caught his interest—I couldn't see what—but all he said was, "New translation project?"

I stuffed the wet book into my satchel and told him a little about it, and then gave him more details about the missing bassoon.

"But really," I said, "you should hear about all this from Nicola."

"Perhaps we can meet for drinks later today," suggested Albert. "What about six?"

"Fine, except she's not allowed to leave Sandretti's *palazzo*."

"Then I'll come to you." He took Ruskin in hand again. "And now, if you'll excuse me, I have an appointment." He winked again and unfolded his long, thin body from the chair and began to wade in purposeful strides across the wet *piazza*.

After a discreet interval, I left the *piazza* too, using a rather less graceful hopping technique to make my way to higher ground. I went into one of the cafés sheltered by the vast arcades and sat down at a marble-topped table. I ordered another cappuccino and some toast and yogurt. I had a view, not of the Basilica di San Marco itself, a cathedral that looks like a combination of a Turkish bath and the palace of Kublai Khan, but of its dreamlike opalescent reflection in the waters of the huge rectangular *piazza*. I thought, *I'm in Italy. In Venice! And someone else is paying!!* For Nicola, generous to a fault, had managed, probably during dinner, to slip a plump envelope of *lire* inside my satchel, along with a note: CR, *you're a pal*.

The convent school of *Lovers and Virgins* was a thing of the past now, and I was deep into Chapter Three, making notes and getting the feel of the thing. I could see that I was going to have trouble with some of the terminology if I took it on as a translation project.

After her wild ride across the pampas, Maria dismounted and handed the reins to the stable hand. He must be new, she thought. For he did not call her señorita and keep his eyes lowered as most of them did. Instead, he faced her boldly and, with a smile that showed white teeth, murmured, "It is clear that the young lady is an excellent rider, even without a saddle."

She slapped his face. How dare he address her, much less make a comment like that? She was sixteen and no child, though she had spent her life being taught by nuns. She knew what he meant. Ladies did not ride without a saddle. That he should even be imagining . . .

More of this mental and physical flouncing about followed before Maria returned abruptly, accepted her stable hand's apologies and began to help him groom the horse.

It was clear where all this was leading, if not in this chapter, then soon. The horse box was reeking of animal sweat and young lust. But the sexual antics of Maria and the stable boy, at least in terms of vocabulary, were not my concern. It was all the unfamiliar and arcane equestrian terms that were throwing me. The author had probably dug them up in some eighteenth-century volume in an obscure private library in a *hacienda* in deepest Venezuela. I had thought my greatest problem with this book was going to be nun speak; now I could see it might be horse talk.

I flipped open *Bashō in Lima* and began to read it slowly, the way it wanted to be read. Now this would be a challenge to translate, a lovely project full of mystery and poetry and deep feeling. I could feel the language of the book easing my heartbeat, rearranging my brain cells. *These* were the kinds of books that should be published, that should be in the world. No one would probably buy it, it's true. It did not have the words NEW INTERNATIONAL BESTSELLER screaming off its pages as did *Lovers and Virgins*. But if I didn't write a favorable reader's report, it would end up in Simon's trash bin, like so many other novels from other countries that publishers and agents with great hopes tried to market to the English-reading public.

When I first arrived at the city of dreams, the city of my youth, the city of unknown possibilities . . .

Then all that caffeine must have kicked in, because suddenly I was impatient with this modern-day Bashō. Wasn't this text a bit precious, a little self-indulgent? I pretended I was Simon, asking: "But what is the book *about*, Cassandra?"

For an hour or so I went back and forth between the two books, from time to time glancing out the plate-glass windows onto the *piazza*. As the tide receded and the stones of the *piazza* reappeared, the reflection of the basilica vanished. The sun came out, though the mist still lingered in wisps and streamers. The arcades were filling with those tourists who would not be put off by a touch of damp; they were streaming toward the Palace of the Doges and the basilica, toward the Accademia Museum and the Rialto Bridge. Some were simply streaming in circles, already lost and befuddled.

To my surprise, I saw someone I recognized in the crowd. He stood out because of his height. It was big, blond Gunther making his way through the opposite arcade, his head bent as he struggled to listen to whoever was talking to him on his cell phone. But that wasn't what made me hastily jam the books back in my satchel, jump up and dash out the café door . . . It was that Marco was following him.

And Andrew McManus was following Marco.

Four

I UNDERSTAND there are many detective novels set in Venice. If I were a thriller writer, it's the one place I would avoid. Venice can never be described too often. On the other hand, I was discovering the practical problems of investigation in this city of bridges and narrow, twisting lanes. It is almost impossible to follow suspects without A) being seen and B) getting lost.

I succeeded for a short while in keeping Andrew's cereal box head in view while I pressed myself into narrow doorways, popped out again and attempted to hide, very unconvincingly, behind passersby, most of whom seemed to be shorter than I. The only things I had going for me were that Andrew was watching Marco follow Gunther, and none of the three had turned around.

Nevertheless, before too much time had passed, I took a wrong turn and lost them all. I thought I might be near the Rialto Bridge; I was in a dense thicket of touristy shops full of glass objects and rather hideous masks of silver-and-white leather topped with feathers and costume jewelry. In the midst of all this was a *fornaio*, a bakery, so I stopped and had a slice of pizza to settle my nerves, and while I ate it I looked in the window of the stationery shop next door. At first I dismissed it as another touristy place, one of the many shops that sold marbled papers and bound books. But gradually I weakened and admitted to myself that I would love to have the money to write letters on mold-made Fabriano paper using a glass pen with a steel nib dipped in tinted ink. To tell the truth, it was the bottles of ink that really enthralled me. Squat or slender, with hand-lettered labels and caps secured with wax and colored ribbon, they glowed dimly in shades of indigo, burgundy and sepia. I never fool myself that, in an earlier century, I would have been a woman of letters (I would have been keeping pigs in the west of Ireland), still I could dream.

Pens and paper are romantic; a woman with a crust of pizza in her hand and a dab of tomato sauce on her face is not. I suddenly saw my reflection in the glass and, behind it, the figure of a young woman looking curiously at me. Her twisted-up pile of red-gold hair and her pale face with its prominent thin nose made me understand Ruskin's claim that Venetians were Gothic, not Renaissance. She was wearing a white, long-sleeved shirt with a crisp high collar; she had an almost monastic appearance.

Well, I can look, can't I? I thought defensively. Then a surprisingly mischievous grin lit her austere face, and I went in.

We exchanged *buon giornos* and a few other pleasantries about the weather and what a lovely shop, yes, in the family for three generations, and then she asked me if I was Spanish.

"Irish," I said, then amended, "North American," and amended again, "But I travel a lot. My Italian sounds Spanish because I'm a translator."

"And whom have you translated?" she asked. Her eyes were the green of sunlight in the forest. She was probably twenty years younger than I was, but if I never took off my beret—a handsome second-hand Canadian Mounties' affair—she wouldn't see my gray hair. I had been told that my chin was holding up admirably, and certainly my spirit had always been that of an adolescent (I had been told that often enough too).

"Gloria de los Angeles. Luisa Montiflores. Elvira Montalban. My own name is Cassandra Reilly." I wrote it on the scratch pad in a flourish of sepia.

"Francesca," she said and then told me she didn't much care for the overblown magic realism of Gloria de los Angeles and had never heard of Luisa Montiflores, the Uruguayan writer whose latest novel, *Diary of a First Love in Montevideo*, had just won a prize whose monetary worth would keep her in paper and pencils for perpetuity. Fortunately Francesca was a great fan of Elvira Montalban, the Argentinean author whose career I had in a sense invented.

"You're her translator? You know Elvira Montalban?"

"I knew her from the beginning. Before the beginning, in fact."

Trading on the glamour of my profession, I casually dropped the fact that I had other interests here in Venice than a mere working holiday. "Music is another passion of mine. I especially love the bassoon."

"Bassoon?" she said, for I had used the English word.

"*Fegato*," I said, and then remembered that was liver.

Francesca burst out laughing. "*Fagotto!*"

I leaned forward confidentially. "I'm really here to help a friend of mine who has been accused of stealing a very old bassoon. A bassoon originally from the Pietà."

Francesca looked sober. "That is terrible, if she stole it."

"Of course she didn't steal it. Someone else has stolen it, and they're blaming it on her, and she's being kept prisoner in some *palazzo* by a man called Marco Sandretti and his father."

"Sandretti?" Francesca's pale face flushed. "I have a friend called Sandretti. She works in a music shop. Roberta is her name. Her brother is Marco. But she doesn't get along with her family."

"A music shop: perfect," I said. "She'll know all about musical instruments. Does she play anything?"

"She plays the clarinet in a group. She also plays in the Piazza San Marco at night. But, yes, she will know about old bassoons. I will take you to see her. We can go now." Francesca rose gracefully and went into the back room, where she had a slightly heated discussion with someone. A woman—undoubtedly Francesca's mother—with dyed red hair and a severe expression returned with her.

Francesca and I set off through the tangled streets and, as we walked, I told her a little about *Lovers and Virgins*, which seemed suddenly to be weighing down my satchel.

"It's overheated, but effective," I said. "She certainly can write a love scene." I hated to admit it, but the predictably sweaty events in the horse stall had been rather arousing. *Cassandra's skin was aflame with the nearness of Francesca. Although they had met only a few minutes before, Cassandra felt an inner insistent throbbing that told her that her life had utterly changed.*

Perhaps that was going too far, but I did feel unsettled and I didn't think it was just the pepperoni pizza. I couldn't tell if Francesca felt anything at all, though she constantly turned to me with a smile I chose to read as promising.

When we got to the music shop, it turned out that Roberta wasn't working that day, but was practicing at home with her group.

"Come tonight to the Piazza San Marco," invited Francesca. "We'll have a drink outside and listen to her, and then you can ask her any questions you like."

"Fine," I said and then hesitated, "I wonder if I could take you to lunch? You've been so helpful."

"I would love to, but I must get back to the shop. My mother already thinks I'm lazy and looking for excuses not to work. I don't want to work there, you see, I want . . . to be a writer."

She flushed and gave me a quick kiss on the cheek. "I am so happy I met you today," she said. "We'll see each other again tonight, after ten, and you can tell me all about the famous writers you know. Elvira Montalban, I'm so impressed! Her first novel, *The Academy of Melancholy*, is just the kind of book I'd like to write someday."

I sighed as she moved off through the crowds. *Francesca had been gone only a moment and yet Cassandra longed for her with all the force of her being.*

I decided to head back to the Sandretti's *palazzo* and see if Marco would allow me to take Nicky out to lunch. I wanted to pump her for more information. Then she and I would meet Albert for drinks at six to learn if any antique black-market bassoons were floating about. At eight was a concert performance of Vivaldi's opera *Orlando Furioso* at the Pietà. Andrew had said that Miss de Hoog was participating in it; he had given me to understand, with a sigh, that her oboe-playing left something to be desired. I gathered that declining to attend was not an option. Afterwards I planned to head over to the Piazza San Marco to hear Marco's sister, Roberta, play the clarinet. And to see Francesca again.

When I arrived at the Sandretti's *palazzo*, it was later than I'd expected. I'd boarded the wrong *vaporetto* and found myself going the long way around to the Záttere. To my surprise, no one answered the door. Perhaps Marco had taken them all off somewhere, either for lunch or to a rehearsal. I suddenly remembered that Gunther, Marco and Andrew had been following each other around the city earlier this morning. Meeting Francesca had put it entirely out of my mind.

What had they been doing?

I went back to my hotel and lay down on the bed for a second that turned into two hours. When I finally woke, I felt disoriented and vaguely troubled. The mists of the morning had solidified into humid heat so that even when I flung open my window on the canal, the air that entered seemed no fresher than what was in my room. I didn't have a headache exactly, more like a pressure hovering around my temples. A straight espresso was what I needed, I decided. I splashed some water on my face, rubbed at the creases in my skin from the bedspread, and set out for a café.

Some ominous feeling was in the air, or in my blood. A strong dose of java helped clear my head, but not my mood. I walked the few blocks over to the *palazzo* in a languid state. Coming from inside the house was the unmistakable *pop-pop-pop* of two bassoons racing each other through a Baroque score. But even that normally cheerful repartee sounded anxious.

The downstairs door was unlocked, so I walked in. I could hear someone in agitated conversation upstairs. Then Marco appeared at the top of the staircase and rushed toward me, followed by the ever-helpful Andrew.

"Where is she? Where has she gone?"

"Who?"

"Nicky. Nicola. Miss Gibbons." He gave it a soft G, as in gibberish.

"Why are you asking me? You were supposed to be watching her. If you were worried she might leave then what were you doing wandering around the Piazza San Marco late this morning with Gunther and Andrew?"

Marco ignored that, though I saw Andrew flinch slightly. "The police took her passport," Marco said, "so she cannot leave the country by air. She could be in any city in this country. Where would we look?"

"This just proves she took the bassoon, Marco," Andrew said.
Marco shook his head. "I cannot believe that."

"Of course she took it," said Bitten, strolling down the stairs, carrying the bassoon she'd been playing, a huge dark thing with many shiny keys. She looked cool and unruffled, but there was a stain on the front of her blouse and an overheated glint far back in her eyes. "And now may the rest of us get on with our lives? Gunther and I both have flights out early tomorrow. I hope you will not try to detain us."

"This is dreadful, dreadful mess," moaned Marco. "I just called my father. He is arriving soon. He will kill me."

"There now," said Andrew, taking the opportunity to throw a powerful arm over Marco's shoulder. "No need to get so worked up. It's not your responsibility. It never should have been. It's a job for the . . . ." His eyes flicked over to my Canadian Mounties' beret, "the *carabinieri*. They'll find her, Marco."

For once Marco seemed to welcome Andrew's solicitous arm.

"Where's Gunther?" I asked.

"Cleaning his bassoon no doubt," said Bitten.

"So I gather the two of you have been together most of the afternoon," I said.

"We need to practice a lot."

"I saw Gunther this morning in the *piazza*."

"He had to change some money."

"You weren't with him."

"I was getting my hair done." Bitten growled at me. "Then we had lunch out. We came back around three, and then . . . ." Gunther came downstairs, yawning, his lips loose and wet.

"Who saw Nicola today?" I demanded.

They all looked at each other.

"She had breakfast in her room," said Marco. "She didn't open

39

the door. She said she didn't feel well. She was going to sleep."

"That's when you felt secure enough to go following Gunther," I said.

"Following me?" Gunther said with surprise. "Who? Why?"

Marco and Andrew exchanged a glance. I started to say something, but stopped at the sound of footsteps on the walk. Let it be her, let it be just a question of Nicky's escaping briefly for a bit of exercise.

"This look familiar, anyone?" said Albert Egmont, walking in the door like a traveling Giacometti statue, weedy and existential, carrying a long paper parcel. When he unwrapped the package, it proved to be a large wooden tube that doubled halfway down. It had only a few holes, no keys and a battered-looking mouthpiece.

"Where, where did you find that?" Marco whispered. He took it quickly, but with reverence. "Who are you?"

"Albert is a . . . friend of mine," I explained.

"Not exactly your type, I would have thought," Bitten muttered. She had been strangely nonplussed by the sight of the bassoon, and it was clear she wanted to stretch out a hand and examine it more closely. Something held her back.

"Cassandra, my dear," said Albert. "I'm really at a bit of a loss. This was hardly the reception I was expecting. Can anyone explain what's going on? Perhaps we should begin with mutual introductions."

I wanted to get through it quickly, but Albert insisted on shaking everyone's hand. I noticed that more than one person could barely repress a desire to rub off the feel of the black leather glove afterward.

"Now," he said, but at that moment an extremely handsome older man came rushing up the walkway, calling angrily to Marco. The man was obviously his father. He was followed by Anna de Hoog.

She looked even dustier and more self-effacing than usual next to Signore Sandretti, who was stuffed into an expensive suit. His head sat on his shoulders like a Roman bust on a well-upholstered pillar.

He ignored us and began grilling his son in low rapid Italian. I couldn't hear all of it, but judging from the miserable look on Marco's face, it was clear his father held him completely responsible for Nicky's disappearance.

"Now see here," said Andrew to Signore Sandretti. "Your son can't be faulted in any way. It's a full-time job guarding someone as determined as Nicola Gibbons. If you were so concerned about her getting away with the bassoon, you should have had her arrested and taken to jail."

"Good riddance to bad rubbish, that's what I say," Bitten said. She'd gotten hold of the period bassoon and was examining it with feigned casualness.

Gunther, as usual, appeared completely preoccupied with dreamy thoughts of his own. I was struck by the fact that, though he was in his thirties, no worry lines etched his smooth face. I had hardly heard him say a word besides *Ia, ja, Frigga* since I'd arrived.

"What's all this?" said Albert to me.

"The friend I told you about, Nicky, seems to have bolted."

"Dear, oh dear," said Albert, taking back the bassoon, a little peremptorily, from Bitten.

"But at least the bassoon has been returned," said Anna de Hoog.

Signore Sandretti stopped his interrogation of Marco and turned his full attention to the instrument in Albert's hands.

"I have never seen this instrument in my life," he repeated in slow, correct English. He handed it back to Albert with a show of dramatic contempt that could not quite disguise his curiosity. "May I ask where you obtained this bassoon?"

"I have it on good authority," said Albert, "that this instrument came on to the market just a day or two ago."

"Which market?" asked Andrew, who had been staring steadily at Albert.

"Oh, come now," said Albert, with a slight smile. "You don't really expect me to reveal my connections?"

Signore Sandretti turned angrily and went upstairs. He unlocked a door and I had a quick glimpse of what seemed to be a magnificent library. Soon we heard him talking in a low and persuasive voice on the telephone.

"Are we dismissed now?" asked Bitten.

"Please, no," said Marco unhappily. "My father says, please, all stay together. We will have a small dinner and then go to the Pietà for the performance tonight. You are invited too, Mrs. Reilly. And your friend, Mr. Egmont."

I noticed that both Andrew and Bitten looked as if the notion of Albert joining us was not terribly appealing. Andrew, in fact, was still lightly rubbing together the fingers that had touched Albert's.

"Of course, Albert and I would love to join you all."

"I beg you not to go further with that *fagotto*," said Marco. "We will leave it here in a locked room."

"If you'll excuse my saying so," said Albert, "the security here leaves something to be desired. I'll hold on to it for now." He wrapped the bassoon back up in paper and tied it firmly with string.

Five

"WHY ARE THE PLOTS of old operas so complicated?" I complained as I attempted to understand the synopsis of *Orlando Furioso*. We were in the Church of the Pietà waiting for the performance to begin. It was a simple church, not terribly large, with a minor Tiepolo on the ceiling, and upper side balconies covered by grille work. The choir had sung, semi-hidden, behind the grilles. Long ago the orphan girls, cloistered and modest, could have sung up in the balconies, but the orchestra must have been here below, just like tonight. They would have needed to be close to their red-haired conductor Vivaldi.

"Eighteenth-century audiences never paid attention to the plot during the performance," Andrew told me. "They listened to the arias, but they would talk during the *recitativos*, which carried the plot along. That's why the librettist wrote an introduction for the libretto. It could be as complicated as he and the composer wanted, yet they didn't worry that the audience would jump up in the middle and say, 'What's really going on here?'"

"Vivaldi, he loved the opera," said Marco. "Here he was, so

famous as a violinist and composer at the Pietà, but he wrote many, many operas as well. About forty or eighty. It's always very confusing though, his operas. Everybody love the somebody who is not the real somebody. Everybody is pretending: *he is my brother, not my lover,* you know. Or they find out the servant is their son or grandfather."

"Of course," said Andrew. "Throughout European history, children were constantly being abandoned by their true parents and brought up by others. Before the foundling hospitals in the Renaissance, people would just leave their babies in trees or by fountains and expect that someone would pick them up and take them home. It would then be a likely occurrence that people turned out to be related."

"Yes, and sometimes in the operas," added Marco, "the women are men and the men are women. Everybody is in disguise, and love must be secret."

There was a slight sigh from Andrew. Some love was not that secret. In front of us were Bitten and Gunther, cooing and grunting. Marco's father was offstage, but I could see Miss de Hoog holding her oboe somewhat awkwardly while she chatted with one of the violinists. She was wearing a sleeveless black dress that made me realize her arms were indeed quite muscular.

It was not a staged opera, of course, not in such a small space. When the lights dimmed, the soloists filed in, the women in deeply cut evening gowns. The part of Orlando, which must have been sung by a castrato in the eighteenth century, was to be sung by a mezzo. The soloists stood there during the overture, trying to look rapturous. Then the action began. Orlando was not yet furious, but hopeful, singing to his lost Angelica.

I was paying attention during the first aria or two, but sometime after that, all the music began to blend together, the way Vivaldi's compositions often did with me. Although I thought of Vivaldi as easier on the ears than Bartók, I couldn't always distinguish between repetition and variation in the Baroque master's style. I began thinking about Nicky instead, wondering where she was and what she was keeping from me. I didn't think she was in any danger, but so far she'd been less than forthcoming. There was a mystery here that was not just about a missing bassoon, and it irritated me that she hadn't confided what it was. What were we to each other, especially now that Olivia was gone?

Since Olivia's death, Nicky had been urging me to move into one of the three bedrooms in the Hampstead house. She wouldn't come right out and say she was lonely—"It's ridiculous for you to hide up there in the attic when I'm rattling around in this bloody huge mansion by myself"—just as I wouldn't come out and say that the prospect of leaving my attic room was seductive but terrifying.

"You should let out the rooms," I urged her instead. "Think of all the young musicians who'd love such a nice house to live in. After all, I'm hardly in London."

And to prove it, shortly after Olivia's funeral, I'd gone off first for a month to Argentina and then for an extended stay to Sydney, where I'd met Dr. Angela Notion. Translation projects hadn't taken me to the South Seas. I said it was my romance with Angela of the Turtle Eggs, but in fact it was fear of Nicky's need for me. And how secretly pleased I'd been when I returned to find Nicky just leaving for Venice. It had meant I could enjoy all the nice things in her house while at the same time ensconcing myself firmly in the attic so that when she returned, there'd be no question of my moving downstairs. I'd grown up with a houseful of sisters, after all, and privacy, even uncomfortable privacy, was the joy of my adulthood.

Suddenly the first act of *Orlando Furioso* was over, and I still didn't know what he was so upset about.

"She is dreadful. This Anna de Hoog is truly dreadful," Andrew said in a vehement voice barely disguised by the clapping around us. "Did you see the way the conductor glared at her when she hit that B flat? Why the devil did your father invite her?" he asked Marco.

Marco shrugged unhappily, as Albert excused himself and left our row. I had noticed that Marco seemed to take upon himself the weight of situations that had nothing to do with him.

"Do you play an instrument, Marco?" I asked.

"Me? Oh no. Nor my father, either. But he was singing opera when he was younger. A tenor. Now he just organizes. Me, too. It is other people who have the talent for music."

I'd warmed to Marco immediately, but it was hard to appreciate Andrew. He seemed to have little of the ironic self-deprecation I enjoyed so much in his fellow Canadians. But perhaps he was just insecure. He reminded me a little of a French teacher I'd had in junior high, a toupéed older man with an execrable accent (I knew this because I later reproduced it in Paris, to looks of great horror), who showed us slides of his trips to France. In these slides one or more handsome young sailors always seemed to be lurking in the background.

Gunther and Bitten turned around, two blue-eyed giants in love. The dazed expression on their faces was too much to bear in duplicate.

Andrew said to them, in real anguish, "It's an insult to Vivaldi," and Gunther nodded solemnly, while keeping his arm firmly around Bitten. Bitten said, "I've been trying to understand. Is it that the acoustics are so bad, or is it the orchestra? Surely *we* did not sound so bad as they."

"It's not the acoustics," said Andrew, and I was amazed at how violent his feeling was. "The singers are really dreadful too. The whole performance is intolerable."

I wanted to say that I didn't think it was so bad, but I knew they wouldn't be interested in my opinion. I was relieved to see Albert threading his way back among the returning members of the audience.

"But where is the bassoon?" Marco asked.

"I thought it best to put it in a safer place, not far from here."

"What safer place?" Marco said, but in a lower tone, and in Italian, for that was the language Albert had addressed him in.

They murmured back and forth, but loud enough so that all of us, including Bitten and Gunther, could hear the word *Danieli*.

The Danieli was one of the poshest hotels in Venice, and it was practically right next door to the Pietà. Could Albert possibly be staying there?

The second act began with a flourish. I had, in spite of my best intentions, been unable to recall the plot, so I was soon at sea. In a Baroque vessel sailing in alternately splashy and calm waters of the human soul, yearning, restless and joyful.

Beside me, Albert and Marco listened intently, but I heard Andrew sighing in disgust, presumably at ear-bending oboe errors that I couldn't recognize. The rest of the audience seemed quite enthralled. At least until, during a solemn moment, the sound of a cell phone trilled as demandingly as a tiny poodle wanting to be picked up.

It was Gunther's Handy. He answered it in a low voice, at the same time rising to excuse himself. Of course he was in the middle of the row. From the set of Bitten's shoulders, it was clear she wasn't at all happy, and after a few minutes, just as everyone in her church pew got settled again, she popped up like an extremely large jumping jack and pushed her way out after Gunther.

The concentration of the singers and players faltered, particularly after the second interruption (for some reason Bitten felt compelled to say *Scusi* several times in a distractingly loud voice, especially after she half-fell onto the lap of an elderly man who had been snoozing), and although the musicians went on with as much verve as possible, Andrew's critical, pained sighs increased.

At the next interval Marco got up, murmuring, "I must tell Gunther to turn off his telephone." A moment or two later, Andrew followed him out.

Albert and I remained where we were. When the rows around us had emptied, I said, "It's quite unusual that two bassoons should go missing at the same time, don't you think?"

"Highly unusual," said Albert, "and, in fact, quite untrue."

"What do you mean, untrue?"

"It's the same bassoon all right."

"But Signore Sandretti . . ."

"One might ask oneself why."

"Did you get the strong impression that Bitten recognized it?"

"Yes. But for some reason she didn't want to say anything."

"Marco thought the bassoon was the right one," I pointed out.

"But after his father said it wasn't, Marco immediately fell in line."

"What about Andrew?"

"His face reveals nothing most of the time except a great eagerness to be with Marco. But no, I'm tempted to believe that he didn't steal it. Nor did Gunther."

"Why would Signore Sandretti . . .?"

"That remains to be discovered. Meanwhile the bassoon is safe."

"At the Danieli?"

Albert smiled, but all he said was, "Ah, so you can eavesdrop in Italian too. A useful skill."

None of our friends returned for the opening of Act Three, a truancy I'm sure the performers appreciated. Perhaps it was the absence of a critical voice next to me, but from the opening strains I began to hear and feel the music this time. In spite of the hard pews and less than perfect acoustics, the singing began to penetrate my bones with intense sweetness. Festive, sober, giddy, tragic, the music floated me down rivers and danced with me in mirrored reception rooms. I closed my eyes, and when I opened them again, I glimpsed for just a second a world other than the superficial and tawdry one I lived in. It was not a perfect place, of course, for it was created by human beings who loved intrigue, complexity, luxury and revenge. Emotionally, it was not a simpler world, but it was one that was livelier and more dignified. I opened my eyes and saw a richly intricate Guardi painting superimposed over the church scene. Instead of a motley collection of tourists dressed in T-shirts and jeans, I saw silk dresses, velvet capes, embroidered breeches and stockings. I smelled sweat and heavy perfume, candle wax and damp stone. Behind the latticed balconies, the voices of the chorus poured out like water. And the orchestra of women below was filled with beautiful orphaned musicians looking pale and monastic. Like Francesca.

The presentation was over and everyone took a bow, many more bows, actually, than necessary. As Albert and I got up to go, I saw Bitten in a side pew, alone. Outside the church we found Marco and Andrew leaning against a balustrade. Marco was having a nervous smoke and didn't meet my eyes. I hadn't seen him smoke before.

"Where's Gunther?" Bitten asked Marco, coming up behind us. "Didn't he come back yet?"

"Come back from where?" Albert asked.

"Oh, he took a walk. He was feeling rather restless," Bitten said, after a pause in which she seemed to take hold of herself. "I'm sure he'll meet us soon."

If that was the case, then why did she suddenly sound so nervous?

I was eager to dump the bassoonists after the concert, but they insisted on clumping together like amoebas under a microscope. No one spoke. As we walked away from the Pietà, Bitten kept looking around for Gunther, and Andrew and Marco seemed suddenly shy with each other. I wondered if Andrew had gotten a little of what he wanted. At the door of the Hotel Danieli, one of the doormen gave a respectful wave to Albert. So he *was* staying there.

Albert swung along beside me, bowler low on his forehead, trousers too short above black boots that caught the shine of the street light above. He whistled a tune between his teeth, but it wasn't from the Vivaldi opera we'd just heard. It was *Between the Devil and the Deep Blue Sea*, and it echoed the clarinet solo we were heading toward. He moved to take my arm, and although I shuddered slightly at his touch, I allowed it. Not for the first time did I wonder about Albert's sexual proclivities. He was such an enigmatic blend of innocence and cunning, he could turn out to be either chaste or polymorphously dissolute. The only thing I didn't believe about Albert was that he was happily married and lived with a wife and two children in the bucolic English countryside.

The air was still humid, and the sky was heavy and moonless; each breath I took tasted of musty salt, of old wood and damp stone. As I had in the Pietà, I closed my eyes and opened them again, imagining myself in an earlier time, when masked women in wide cloaks stepped into gondolas, the gondolas that now rode emptily in their moorage in the wide basin to our left.

Marco caught up to me and Albert. He seemed worried that we were headed in the direction of Piazza San Marco and in the direction of the clarinet.

"We take the *vaporetto* over to Accademia," he reminded me.

"A nightcap, yes?"

"You can do what you like. I don't believe I'm under any sort of obligation to spend all my time with you lot."

"No, of course not," murmured Marco unhappily as we arrived at the square.

"How the heck should I know where he is?" Andrew was now saying under his breath to Bitten. "You're the ones who had the lovers' quarrel."

"We . . ."

"Bitten, I *heard* you two arguing."

"Where?"

But then they both noticed I had stopped abruptly and seemed to be listening to them.

I did hear them, but I had stopped for quite another reason. I had seen, alone at an outdoors café table, a figure with red-gold hair in a dark coat that was pulled tightly around her shoulders. She was enthralled by the trio directly in front of her, especially by the young woman who was similar enough to Marco to be his twin. Roberta Sandretti. The same straight nose, decisive brows, dark curly hair. But she radiated a kind of energy that made her brother look like a low-wattage light bulb. Her eyes flashed the intelligence of their father, along with the joyful controlled abandon of a real musician.

I assumed Francesca had told Roberta about me, for she looked me over boldly as she lowered her clarinet for a moment. Boldly and with the practiced eye of someone assessing the competition.

We seated ourselves and ordered overpriced drinks from a waiter who had no right to look contemptuous, considering how few people made the step from mildly interested strolling passerby to paying customer.

The set ended—perhaps a little sooner than the bass player and pianist had expected—and Roberta bowed briefly to acknowledge our applause before coming over. She pulled up a seat between me and Francesca and kissed her cheek.

We were introduced all around.

"But, of course, I know *him*," she said, waving dismissively at her brother.

Francesca said to me, "I told her about the missing bassoon . . ."

I smiled to show it would be best not to get into *that* discussion immediately, and asked Roberta where she'd studied.

At the Conservatory of Music, she told me. "Along with Marco. But now I work in a music shop, and he is an errand boy for my father."

She seemed to be deliberately taunting him. He said something in dialect I couldn't quite catch, and she answered him just as rapidly with a rude gesture in the direction of Andrew, who had an arm draped over the back of Marco's chair.

Marco jumped up. Roberta jumped up. Francesca looked proud but alarmed, Andrew confused, Bitten preoccupied. Only Albert thought to intervene. Holding out a black-gloved hand like a policeman, he blew on an imaginary whistle. He followed this by a short, graceful speech in Italian about there being a time and a place for everything.

Roberta turned her back on us and walked up to her place by the piano, and Marco sat down dejected, but not before I'd had a chance to see the expression of fury distorting his handsome face. He rather violently pushed away Andrew's consoling hand on his shoulder.

Our drinks arrived, and Andrew insisted on paying. "We're in Venice," he said, with an imploring look at Marco. "On a beautiful night."

That probably made about as much sense to Marco as it would saying to someone from Winnipeg, "We're in Winnipeg, let's enjoy ourselves!"

But it *was* a gorgeous night, and the *piazza was* magic, and Roberta wasn't glaring at me as I edged my chair slightly closer to Francesca's; she was launching into something wild that had more klezmer in it than Benny Goodman.

Bitten said, "Do you hear a siren?"

A police boat was speeding across the water in the direction of the Pietà.

Six

I DIDN'T SEE Anna de Hoog at first. She was surrounded by Italian police, gondoliers and porters from the Danieli Hotel. But the big, blond body that had been dragged from the canal was clearly recognizable. We didn't need Bitten's scream to tell us it was Gunther.

The narrow canal that runs by the hotel is one of the busier waterways in Venice. In addition to gondolas, private cruisers and barges loaded with goods, water taxis were constantly arriving and departing from the small dock next to the hotel. From where we stood, on the stone bridge over the canal, the dock was inaccessible. You would have to go through the hotel to get to it, which Bitten did. The rest of us remained on the bridge.

Andrew looked pale. He leaned over the bridge and was sick over the side. Marco patted his shoulder distractedly and went over to the group down on the short strip of quay opposite the hotel, a group I could now see included Signore Sandretti. Across the canal, on the hotel's landing dock, the unremarkable Anna, still in her formal black dress, was in the center, apparently explaining who

Gunther was. Bitten knocked her aside in her haste to get at the corpse of her lover.

Francesca and Roberta came racing up to me on the bridge and gasped when they saw Gunther's body laid out on the dock.

"Who is he?"

"The German bassoonist," I said. "I wonder if it was the oboist, Anna de Hoog, who discovered him."

Signore Sandretti glanced up and noticed us standing on the bridge above. A look of distaste, even rage, crossed his face when he saw his daughter with Francesca. It reminded me of Marco's expression just a short while earlier, when handsome turned to horrifying for a split second. Roberta returned his glare with vigor, but I felt Francesca tremble slightly beside me.

It soon became obvious that we could do nothing. Marco returned from a conversation with the police and said we should all go home; the inspector would let us know in the morning if he needed a statement from any of us. For the moment the police were treating Gunther's death as suspicious, but only after an autopsy would they be able to pinpoint the cause. They would interview Miss Johansson and Miss de Hoog now.

"But how did it happen?" I whispered to Marco in Italian. "Did Anna de Hoog see anything?"

"No, she left the Pietà immediately after the performance and came into the Danieli to meet someone for a drink. There was a commotion on the dock, and she went out and was able to identify Gunther."

Marco looked subdued and scared. He avoided looking down at his father. I wondered if Sandretti would hold Marco responsible. Roberta left the bridge without speaking to her brother, and Francesca, giving me a shaky smile, trailed after her.

I cast one last glance at the scene below, with Bitten collapsed like a fallen Valkyrie at the feet of a slain warrior companion, and then reluctantly followed Marco and Andrew to the *vaporetto* stop and back across the Grand Canal to the Dorsoduro. No one had mentioned the word *murder* yet, but it lingered in the air like the brackish scent of the canals.

I couldn't help thinking, *It's unfortunate that Nicky had to choose this afternoon to disappear.* And that made me remember that Albert Egmont had not been among those who had arrived breathless at the scene of the crime. The last time I remembered seeing him was at the table in the *piazza,* with a Campari in front of him and a look of pleasure on his austere face as he tapped his black fingers in time to the clarinet.

The next morning I woke from a dream of stone echoing under a solitary step. The sound was coming from outside my hotel, but the steps wound their way into my sleep. I was in a convent, a nun, and in my dream it was a very pleasant thing. I had no worries and no job other than to walk in circles and pray. No romantic entanglements complicated my life; my yearning was only for the Virgin. Best of all, I knew I was making my mother happy. She had longed to be a nun herself, she'd once confided, and had hoped that one of her four daughters would make the choice. I was the least likely of the four to take the veil; on the other hand, I was the only girl in the family who was still technically a virgin, which counted for something I suppose.

I'd ordered my breakfast brought up and in great luxury sat up in bed with a tray of rolls and fruit and coffee, with *Lovers and Virgins* open in front of me. It was gray and overcast outside, and I was in no hurry to go out. Nicky might or might not show up, with or without explanations or bassoons. Gunther's death might or might not be solved. But in the timeless world of a romance novel, life would go on, like a ship surging over rhythmic waves of luxurious prose. Despite some feeling of guilt on my part, *Bashō in Lima* had migrated to the small pile of books I'd brought with me but hadn't yet opened. Guilt, because I knew it was real literature, composed with thoughtfulness and intent. Guilt, because I considered myself a literary person, widely read and not adverse to working my way down through the surface of a text to the meaning below.

I couldn't help it, though, I *had* to find out what was happening to the four sisters in Venezuela.

I had come to the part where Lourdes, the baby of the family, was demanding to return to the convent and become a novice. She had seen her sister Maria's seduction by the stable hand, and her innocent mind had rebelled and turned it into a Biblical vision that she kept babbling about, much to Maria's dismay. Mercedes, her next oldest sister, who clearly had her wits about her and was perfectly aware of what had gone on in the horse box, was considering taking the veil as well. Not because she completely believed in God or thought that locking herself up in a nunnery was so fabulous, but because the convent had a library, and the library contained not only the complete works of Voltaire and Rousseau, but also Mary Wollstonecraft's *A Vindication of the Rights of Woman*, books she couldn't obtain elsewhere. As Mercedes said, "What else can a woman with a mind do in this godforsaken country but live as a nun?"

Occasionally my mind drifted to the Ospedale della Pietà and to the musicians there. Had the orphanage been a kind of prison where musicians were produced for the entertainment of the Venetian nobility and foreign guests? Or had it been a safe haven where girls who would have otherwise been on the streets were assured of education and livelihood, where talent was recognized and rewarded? What if my choice had been between cloistered musical servitude and prostitution? What would I have chosen? Nun, I thought, but crossed my fingers behind my back. Shut away, but at least with my own kind. Maybe some of the Pietà girls were the same kind of virgin I was. Maybe, I liked to think, they had had time for a kiss in between all those hours of practicing the bassoon.

There was a knock at the door and the maid came in. I'd been in bed most of the morning, and I assumed she probably wanted to make up the room; instead, she handed me an envelope with my name on it.

I opened it quickly.

Cassandra. Meet me at one at the Campo Santa Margherita at the Bar Antico.

N.

P.S. Don't tell anyone where you're going or let yourself be followed.

"Who gave you this?"

The maid smiled and shrugged. "The front desk."

But when I went downstairs a little later, the clerk at the front desk professed not to know anything about it. I asked if anyone else had left me a message, and the clerk pulled out a scrap of paper with a single question scrawled across it:

What orchestra or chamber music group does Miss de Hoog play with?

Could it be from Albert? I had never seen his handwriting before, but it was like him to be curious about the least obvious thing.

I'd hoped to see Anna de Hoog at the *palazzo;* to my relief, she was sitting in the garden with a few newspapers and a book beside her, obviously alone. I pulled up a painted iron chair and sat down beside her. It had turned into a sunny day with bouncy white clouds above.

In the dappled shade Anna's skin looked pale and mottled. Did she have a life-threatening disease? Her expression was a picture of serenity.

I picked up the book. It was *Women Musicians of Venice*. It looked like Nicky's copy. When I turned to the inside cover, I saw that indeed it was. Someone else might have apologized for snooping among Nicky's things, but not the unflappable Anna. With a guileless smile, she said, "Wasn't it kind of Nicola to loan me this book?" and she launched into a discussion of the Venetian welfare state that had created the *ospedali* in the first place.

"They say the reason there were so many abandoned children in Venice was that men were encouraged not to marry, and a huge class of courtesans arose. There was no stigma in giving up a child. The mother would simply place the baby in a sort of revolving door and ring the bell. The nuns would be on the other side to take the baby in, wash it and brand it with the letter *P* for instance, if it was the Pietà that was taking the child in, and then give the baby to a wet nurse. It was quite a system, don't you think? I believe the Pietà still has a sign near where the little revolving door used to be. All the same, don't you think some of those women wondered, when they went to the concerts years later, whether their daughters might possibly be among the performers? And don't you think the daughters wondered too, looking through the grille work out into the audience: *Is my mother here?*"

"Not that this isn't fascinating," I interrupted, "but . . ."

"You're probably wondering about Gunther's death," she said quietly. "It was shocking, a shocking thing to see."

When I looked into her eyes, I saw she truly meant it.

"Do the police know anything more?"

She shook her head. "It's always a bit complicated in Italy when a foreigner dies. Especially when foul play is suspected. I believe his grandmother was contacted last night and has arrived this morning."

"And his wife?"

"He wasn't married."

"But this Frigga he kept talking with on his cell phone . . ."

Anna deliberately looked into the distance. "I had thought to be leaving today, now that the symposium is finished and the performance of *Orlando Furioso* is done. But I suspect I may be staying on a few days."

That reminded me of what I took to be Albert's question, left for me at the front desk. "I suppose you have to leave because you have other musical engagements to fulfill?"

"Yes, of course."

"I didn't catch what orchestra you were affiliated with."

"I am not affiliated, only a fill-in," she said, and seemed so pleased with the assonance that she repeated it. But I could see she was watching me carefully and would not be caught out.

"Now I have a question for you," she said, in a disconcertingly flirtatious voice that contrasted with her bland demeanor and inquisitive eyes. "I find your friend Albert Egmont rather fascinating. I had hoped to see more of him. Is that possible? I understand from Marco that he is staying at the Danieli."

"I don't really know."

"But he is your friend." Again, that false sprightliness.

"More an old acquaintance. He knows about missing things."

"Missing things," she said significantly. "Missing bassoons?"

"Among other things."

"Missing things are a sort of specialty of his?"

"Why, did you lose something?" I didn't mean to be rude, but I didn't for a moment believe in this sudden coyness, especially as regarded Albert.

Anna smiled, and something in her eyes said that it was me she found attractive, not my friend the Egg. This disconcerted me even more.

We were interrupted just then by the arrival of Marco with Andrew and Bitten in tow. They had all been to the police station, Marco explained. To give statements.

"But why?" exclaimed Anna. "You were all at the concert last night. Though all of you did miss Act Three." She laughed almost lightheartedly. "In fact, really, it's only Cassandra and I who managed to stay for the whole performance. Come now, it wasn't that bad, was it?" she said to Andrew, as if she knew exactly what he'd been saying about her oboe-playing.

He turned bright red under his freckles, obviously the sort of person who enjoyed snide gossip more than telling hurtful truths.

Bitten hadn't said a word. Her robust Swedish good looks seemed to have vanished overnight. She walked into the *palazzo*, and Marco looked at Anna severely. "It is no laughing matter, Miss de Hoog. This Gunther, he was very nice, and a good musician too. It is a sad thing, a terrible thing, if he was murdered."

"No one feels that more than I," she said, with a sudden return to seriousness. "I laugh because I am nervous. That is all. Has his grandmother arrived yet?"

"Yes. She is at the police station. And Miss de Hoog, the police wish to interview you again for more details about discovering the body."

"Shall I . . . go to the station?" She looked anxious.

"No, the inspector, he will come here very shortly. Please make yourself comfortable. And you, Cassandra?" Marco turned to me. "Still no word from Nicola?"

"Not a peep," I lied.

"Your friend, this Albert, he did not come back to the scene of the crime with us. I told the police he was living at the Danieli."

61

Marco's tone had become more hushed and urgent. He pulled me aside. "The bassoon, have you any thought where is the bassoon?"

"I believe your father told us very firmly yesterday that the bassoon Albert brought over was *not* the bassoon that had been stolen."

"Yes, I know," Marco murmured unhappily.

"Well then?"

"Even fathers make mistakes," suggested Anna de Hoog, who had moved a little closer to us.

Marco turned on her. "Not my father!"

"Sorry, sorry. No reason for alarm." Anna smiled and backed off.

Sorry, sorry. No reason for alarm. It was what the unknown woman who called me in London had said.

In her room over the garden, Bitten had taken up her bassoon. She played a series of warm-up chords that led into an adagio movement from one of Vivaldi's bassoon concertos. I couldn't have told you which one, but I had heard it often enough, for Nicky loved it too. But Nicky had never played it with such a feeling of loss as Bitten did now.

Seven

THE CAMPO SANTA MARGHERITA is long in shape and a bit shabby, like an old slipper. Tourists don't seem to find it particularly enchanting, or to find it at all, for that matter. Since I was early, I took a seat at an outdoor café and pulled out *Lovers and Virgins*, but my mind wandered. This morning I'd been completely engrossed. But I had passed into self-disgust and disbelief. I used to feel the same about the gossip of my older sisters. They'd come in breathy on Saturday nights, full of stories of girls behaving with unvirtuous abandon (not them!) in the back seats of parked cars, and I'd listen avidly before suddenly experiencing remorse. How could I even think of giving this potboiler a positive review, much less translating it into English? English had enough crappy historical romance novels; we didn't need another one from Venezuela. I thought longingly of *Bashō in Lima*. The unnamed narrator wrote me a poem:

Down narrow streets
I search—

*Have you
abandoned me forever?*

I had a cappuccino and forced myself to read on. The sooner I finished this novel and gave it a scathing critique, the sooner I could get on to the other books in the stack. The eldest sister, admirable Isabella, had taken over the running of the *hacienda* and put down a peasant uprising almost single-handedly through a combination of guile and bravado. Had she arranged that the handsome stable hand would die in the riot? Perhaps not, but Maria blamed her sister for his death. Her pregnancy had just begun to show, and she was inconsolable.

Finally it was time to meet Nicky. The bar she'd directed me to was full of students playing pinball. But there was a back room where depressed-looking young people in black bent over books or leaned together talking intently. Nicola was waiting for me, and as I went toward her I was reminded of the first time we met, many years ago in Islington. It wasn't by chance. An acquaintance from a ship traveling down the Nile to Luxor had mentioned that she had a friend who had a friend named Nicola who might have a spare room.

We were both around thirty then, me under, she over. I'd been knocking around the world for a number of years already and had just begun to make some headway in the world of literary translation. Nicky was already well established as a bassoonist and had been living in Olivia's house for almost a decade. It had been just as Nicky was finishing her music degree that she heard Olivia was looking for a live-in secretary. Nicky applied for the job, seeing it as a temporary occupation while she found her feet in the London music world. It had gradually evolved from a job to a friendship to an attachment strong as family. Olivia had gone from being Nicky's mentor to being her responsibility.

Unlike in temperament—Nicky was bold, fresh, open, and Olivia was often secretive and a bit sulky—they were both passionate about their music, and their lives revolved around practicing, rehearsals and performance. When Olivia's arthritis finally made her put down the bow, at least in regard to the concert stage, she continued to teach. It was only at the very end, a year before her death, that she stopped playing. And even then Olivia had never stopped listening to music.

Olivia and I had nothing in common. In the early years, just after Nicky had impulsively offered me the attic room, Olivia had acted as if I hardly existed. The huge house had two stairways, and it was possible for me to enter and leave through the kitchen and former servants' quarters without seeing Olivia at all. Nicky sometimes chided me, "She won't bite you."

"She doesn't like me. She knows my great-grandparents were peasants."

"Nonsense," said Nicky. "She thinks you're a fascinating person. She often asks me where you've been and what you've been up to."

That was a kind lie on Nicky's part. Far from "not biting," Olivia had sharp teeth and exercised them. She had never used them on Nicky, but I had felt their snap often enough. "Oh, Cassandra, dear," she would begin, and I knew some request designed to put me in my place would follow. "If you're going to eat fried fish, could you please not eat it in *my* kitchen? It lin-gers so."

Why did I keep living in her house then, for almost twenty years? It was free, for one thing, thanks to Nicky, and for the most part I really was hardly there. Some years I spent only a month there, other years six months at most. It was an address in a more than respectable part of town (unlike Peckham where I'd previously had a bed sit), an answering service, a steady point in the universe. It allowed me to keep my clothes somewhere, and to have a desk. It allowed me to be attached, but without responsibility.

I stayed there because Nicky wanted me to as well, because Nicky, in spite of all our ups and downs, was a true friend. And perhaps I stayed, too, because of the music.

"I suppose you know that you've gotten yourself in a much worse place than you were in even two days ago." I spoke more harshly than I'd meant to, probably to disguise the wave of sentimentality and relief that had come over me when I saw that she looked fine.

"What do you mean?"

"Gunther's death of course! At first you were only suspected of stealing a period bassoon. Now they think you murdered someone."

"Oh, that's ridiculous. Who killed him? When?" Nicky looked disturbed, but better than I'd seen her two days ago. She was wearing a fitted red sweater with a deep V-neck that showed ample flesh. I knew Nicky was more likely to go for clinging cleavage when she felt she'd pulled off something clever. Her appetite had returned too, if the array of dishes in front of her was any indication. There were several sorts of bruschetta, a salad, a dish of olives, panini with cheese and salami, and a glass of wine.

"Last night. A porter at the Danieli found him floating in a canal by the Pietà."

"Well, that's a shame," she said. "I'm sorry. He actually was quite a good bassoonist." She brooded a little, and then said briskly, "Well, it can't be helped if they suspect me. That's the least of my worries." She took a bite of bruschetta.

"The *least* of your worries? May I inquire then, very respectfully, what you *are* worried about? Obviously not your professional reputation."

"It's that horrible Bitten, of course." She pushed a plate toward me and signaled the waiter for another glass of wine and one for herself. "Eat a wee bite, lass. You look starving."

"She's not horrible," I said, remembering Bitten's playing of the adagio movement. "What has she done? Surely you don't suspect her of pushing Gunther in the canal?"

"She told me she's Olivia's granddaughter, that's what she's done."

"What!"

"Bitten asked, after the first morning seminar of the symposium, if I'd like to have a cup of coffee with her. We'd never met, but I was familiar with some of her research on the girls of the Pietà and thought she was trying to connect with me, woman to woman, about the whole notion of Baroque women musicians. We were the only two women in the symposium playing bassoon after all, so it seemed obvious we would want to talk and, I hoped, form an alliance against Mr. Know-It-All McManus. Oh, futile feminist hope!" Nicky finished off another bruschetta.

"To tell the truth, Cassandra, at first I thought she might be putting the make on me, not necessarily because of my gorgeous physique, but because she'd heard of my CD-ROM project, and wanted to be involved. She drew me out, asked me increasingly personal questions about my life in London. You *know* I'm not the most discreet person in the world, Cassandra. It never occurred to me to hide my close relationship with Olivia. I told her all about our long friendship and how Olivia had left me the house and all her possessions and quite a bit of money—I'm afraid, Cassandra, I even exaggerated the amount of money. Vanity, vanity . . ." Nicky drank deeply from her glass.

"But how could Bitten imagine she was related to Olivia? I thought Olivia's son died in a concentration camp during the war."

"According to Bitten, Olivia's son, Jakob Wulf, was married before the war to a girl called Elizabeth. At some point during the war

Elizabeth Wulf, now widowed, made her way to Sweden with Bitten. There she married someone named Johansson, and Bitten grew up thinking he was her father."

"Why has it taken Bitten so long to figure this out? Why now?"

"She says she only just put it together herself," said Nicky. "But I find it impossible to believe that Bitten is any relation to Olivia. There must be some other explanation. Bitten—what kind of Jewish name is that?"

"She's certainly bigger," I said, my imagination jumping back to the photographs in Nicky's study. "But then, Olivia was quite a tall woman in her younger days, and they both have a rather regal tilt to their heads, and the eyes . . . You know, Nicky, I believe their eyes are very similar. Olivia had a very cold stare too."

"I really don't think so," Nicky snapped. "It's a load of codswallop, is what it is."

"Is that what you told her?" I asked.

"Yes. And then she got that very mean, haughty look—which you've *seen*, Cassandra—and said that after all I'd told her about her grandmother, there was good reason to believe the inheritance was really meant for her, and that I'd soon be hearing from her solicitors."

"Oh, no!"

"I said, over my dead body was she getting anything that was rightfully mine, and she said, 'We will see, Nicola Gibbons, we will see,' and that, my dear, is more or less the last real conversation we've had."

Nicky called the waiter over and ordered lemon gelati for both of us, and espresso. I could see that she was shaken by all this, but hardly ready to give in.

"This has been an eventful trip for Bitten then, hasn't it?" I mused. "Didn't her affair with Gunther begin just a few days ago too?"

"The first day," said Nicola. "They were barely introduced when they had their knickers off."

"Who do you think killed him?"

"That Frigga woman, of course. The one he was always talking to on his cellular phone. He told her about his affair, and she came to Venice and pushed him in the canal. Jealousy, pure and simple. It's the second oldest story in the history of humankind."

"What's the first one?"

"Falling in love in the first place."

"Nicky, are you being absolutely honest with me?"

"More or less." But her eyes didn't meet mine.

"Really, I need to know where you've been and what you've been up to. Because you understand that you've put yourself in a rather awkward spot by leaving Venice the day that Gunther was murdered."

"I have a cast-iron alibi."

"And that is?"

"I was playing in a concert in Birmingham, of course. My name is in the program, my splendid notes were heard, my presence was validated by applause."

"The Italian police confiscated your passport! How did you get out of the country and back in again?"

She coughed slightly and produced my Irish passport from a pocket, sliding it over the table toward me.

"But you and I don't look anything alike."

"I told them I'd put on weight. We both have curly hair," she said, digging into her dish of gelato. "Sorry I had to steal your passport, Cassandra, but I really didn't want to quarrel with you about it. Anyway, you have two."

"Is *that* the reason you wanted me to come help you?" I asked, indignant.

"I needed the cash too. I knew that a last-minute, first-class ticket would be expensive. But I knew I'd be less likely to be hassled in first class."

"What about all the other stuff?"

"Moderately useful," she said, but her eyes slid away again.

"Refresh my memory again," I said. "The letter marked PRIVATE was . . ."

"Olivia's will. The money I needed to get to Birmingham. The articles were just backup. The pamphlet had something about the instruments used by the Pietà girls."

"There was also the biography of the conductor."

"Just wanted to check a few facts. What I really need is access to records in Sweden. I suppose . . ." Her eyes fixed on me.

"Don't look at me. I'm through helping you. I thought you needed the money for bribing the Italian officials about that stupid bassoon."

"Oh, yes, the bassoon. Did it ever turn up?"

"A bassoon turned up, but Signore Sandretti said it wasn't the right bassoon. Albert says it is, and I'm inclined to believe him. Of course, no one knows exactly where he is at the moment." I told her about my chance meeting with Albert Egmont and his surprise appearance with a Baroque instrument. Then I went on, because I couldn't help it, to tell her about Francesca and Roberta.

"Marvelous," she said. "I need to meet Roberta immediately. She sounds like the perfect person to help me coordinate the CD-ROM series. I need so much more information about women musicians in Venice."

"What about Bitten? What about the bassoon? What about Gunther? Are you going back to the *palazzo* to get your clothes and things and to tell everyone where you've been?"

"I'll think about it," she said evasively. "At the moment I prefer to lie low for a bit, at least until they've caught up with Frigga. I really can't do much under house arrest, and I need to get started on my research for the CD-ROM. Work out the locations, decide on the music. I need a plot. I'm working on a plot." She looked around for something more to eat, but all the dishes were empty. "Is the divine Bitten still in Venice?"

"Yes. Both she and Gunther had flights out this morning, but of course after his murder she was strongly encouraged not to leave."

"I'll watch out for her then," Nicky said, getting up. "I don't suppose I can borrow your Canadian Mounties' beret? I quite like it."

"Certainly not." I got up too. "Are you at least going to tell me where you're staying? So I can get in touch with you if necessary."

From inside a deep pocket she pulled out a wallet and fished out money for the meal and a card from a small hotel in an alley near the Frari, not far from our bar. "I'm in room seven," she said. "Knock twice."

I hadn't picked up my passport and Nicky took it back. "If you don't mind, I'll keep this awhile."

"The idea that we're anything alike!" I said.

Eight

IT'S POSSIBLE TO WALK more or less directly from the Campo Santa Margherita to the Rialto, but it's far more pleasurable to stroll with the intention—and the time—to get lost. To deliberately turn aside from the signposts that reassure "To the Train Station" or "To the Rialto" in favor of narrow passages that open out into squares with a covered well in the center and laundry hanging from the balconies, where the stones are worn with the feet of centuries and sunlight stripes the ochre and russet walls.

When you're not in a hurry, or in a panic, you have time to see Venetian details: a door knocker shaped like a lion, not the usual Lion of St. Mark, but one that looks more like a monstrous cat; the insignia of the old shoemakers' guild, a little boot, carved into a stone lintel at the far end of the Campo San Tomà. Walking through Venice can be meditative, like walking the labyrinth or traversing a dream map. The folds and passages of Venice resemble those of an old engraving of the brain. A teacher I had once gave us to understand that the brain, uncoiled, unfurled, would take up quantities of space, a seductive and distressing thought to a sixteen-year-old. Venice had that cerebral quality; if all the history crammed and folded and layered into its lagoon-bounded streets and houses and churches were to spread out, it would be infinite.

When I finally arrived at the Rialto market, I was reminded that October is still harvest time in Italy. This afternoon the rain-heavy clouds had lifted, and a drier breeze sailed through the squares where the vendors were coming to the end of their day. The sun put a shine on a pear tomato, the final polish on a speckled zucchini. The fruit stalls displayed pumpkins, figs and grapes, purple, red and citrus-green. Blankets of cilantro, basil and parsley, softened by the warmth of the day, gave off a luxuriant odor that mingled with the faintly brackish water of the nearby canal. Although I wasn't hungry, I lingered at the open door of the pasta shop with its pumpkin-stuffed raviolis and squid black strands of pasta that looked like Halloween fright wigs. I hovered in front of a bakery where thick wicker baskets held six kinds of hand-formed breadsticks and where crackers were the size of placemats. My two books were in my satchel, but although I kept telling myself that any minute I'd find a café (it had to be the right café) and have an espresso and return to my Venezuelan girls, I put it off, block by block, stall by stall. I fought being pulled back into the tangled world of the troubled sisters.

People speak of being a morning person, or a night person; I'm an afternoon soul. I'm most content as the hour approaches four. I didn't discover this until I was an adult and had lived in Spain a year, for afternoons in Kalamazoo, Michigan, where I'd grown up, weren't conducive to contemplation. Four o'clock was the end of the school day, the beginning of chores. But four o'clock in the south of Spain was the time when the sleeping streets began to wake again after the siesta. That languorous awakening (the sound of metal doors rolling back up over storefronts) has stayed with me, has made me love the hour or two of the day when little is expected and nothing can be accomplished.

The serious shoppers were long gone, and the fish market had closed before lunchtime. I bought a cardboard basket of fresh figs and ate them slowly as I walked, sucking at the honey pink flesh through the wrinkled brown skin. Suddenly I saw a back I recognized, a head set boxily on narrow shoulders, a freckled face under a straw boater and sunglasses. I didn't think he was trying to disguise himself. If anything he was acting out a small role from *Death in Venice* or *The Wings of the Dove*.

I followed Andrew over the arch of the Rialto Bridge. At the *vaporetto* stop he noticed me just as the boat docked. We both joined the crush onboard, and the *vaporetto* lumbered off in the direction of Accademia. From the center of the crowd, I couldn't see any of the exquisite palaces along the canal.

"Where are you off to?" Andrew asked the top of my head.

"Nowhere really. I thought I'd just head in the direction of the Lido, maybe get off and have a coffee. Once we get through the Grand Canal, I should be able to get a seat. Or at least get this man's elbow out of my back."

"I wish I could take a break too. I've been looking for a flat to rent, sussing out various leads, but it hasn't been easy. With the symposium and everything . . ." He skipped over last night's events with an unhappy flutter of one hand. "I may end up just renting a room somewhere—if I can even find that. I need to get settled in order to start researching my book. The city has become much more expensive."

"You've been to Venice before?" I asked, resolving, since I was pressed against the length of his body, to take the opportunity to get to know Andrew a little better. Perhaps he could shed some light on what had happened to Gunther.

"I spent a month here as a graduate student. I had *no* money, I

74

had no idea how to meet anybody, but I was happy digging around in the libraries for information on Vivaldi and the *ospedali*. Right from the beginning, I was fascinated by the notion of an orchestra formed of abandoned girls. It's an extraordinary concept when you think about it. All through history children have been rejected and sold by their parents, but generally they ended up as slaves or prostitutes. Perhaps it's because I was adopted myself," he said, "that this subject really drew me."

"Did you know you were adopted? Did they tell you?"

"They didn't tell me, but I suspected," Andrew sighed. "It was obvious that I didn't look like my parents. They were both short and dark-haired, and I had these freckles and towered above them. I didn't know for sure until I was sixteen, but I remember as a child I was fascinated by myths and fairy tales about lineage and family secrets."

"The sort where the King, because of some prophecy, orders the child to be killed, and the Queen or her serving maid gives the baby to shepherds to be brought up, and all the child has is a gold ring, which eventually is recognized?"

"Exactly!" said Andrew. "I loved those fairy tales."

"Me too. What happened when you were sixteen?"

"My parents found me in bed with a neighbor boy. Fortunately my grades were good enough to get me an early admission to university. I got a music scholarship and never looked back."

"You don't see them?"

"No. And you?"

"I keep in touch with one or two of my sisters. My father's dead. I think about my mother sometimes. I want to see her, but I can't imagine it would go well."

"People like us are really the foundlings of the universe. That's what I think. Abandoned by our birth parents, adopted by new kinship groups."

People like us. It had an old-fashioned feel, like Andrew himself. He was too cautious to say *queer* or *gay*.

Gradually we had been pushed into the covered sitting area and had squeezed ourselves onto a bench. We were still plastered together, but at least it was the sides of our bodies touching now, not the fronts. Through the fogged-up windows, stone and plaster palaces wavered in the light thrown up from the canal.

"Ah, Venice!" I said. "Art, music, wine, squid in its own ink, handsome people. Marco's awfully good-looking, isn't he? In that gorgeous, effortless Italian way."

"There probably isn't a single man I know who hasn't dreamed of coming to Italy and finding someone like Marco," Andrew said. "I'm so pleased that I'm going to have a year here with him." It was a slightly more wistful than assured statement.

"But are you sure Marco is . . ."

"Of course he is," said Andrew. "Or at least . . . enough. I mean, it obviously runs in the family—look at his sister."

"And look how Sandretti and Marco treat Roberta. I wouldn't call them exactly supportive."

"Well, I know that Marco likes me, because . . . he kissed me," Andrew blurted, turning bright red under his straw hat. He looked like raspberries and cream. But there was no need to blush; no one around us understood English, or else they didn't care. I wondered if "kissing" was a euphemism, or if it had been really just a kiss, in which case it was rather sweet in these days of graphic grappling.

"Was that during the second interval, when you two were gone?" I put a nice touch of interested sympathy into my voice.

"Yes. I'd been in quite a huff—because of the awful playing and then, on top of that, Gunther's damned cell phone and Bitten causing a giant commotion. You'd think the two of them weren't performers themselves. Not that they interrupted anything very professional. But anyway, I followed Marco out, and we went for a short walk . . ."

"And you saw Gunther. Though not at that point face down in the canal."

"Of course not. He was very much alive. He was with Bitten down by the Naval Museum, and they . . ." Andrew stopped. "Look, it's not my intention to get anyone in trouble."

"I understand."

"I don't think their quarrel was serious anyway. I think she really loved him. Obviously she did when you see how cut up she's been since they found him."

"Oh," I said. "So you and Marco witnessed Bitten and Gunther arguing shortly before he died, is that it? And I suppose that neither of you mentioned this to the police?"

"I don't for an instant believe that Bitten killed him!"

"Why not?"

"Because, well, she wouldn't do that. Aside from obviously adoring him, she's too clever. And it would put a crushing end to her career, wouldn't it? She's a fine Vivaldi scholar. No one has done so much to promote the Baroque bassoon as she has. Yes, *now* people like your friend Nicky are taking up the bassoon concertos, but Bitten has been playing Vivaldi's concertos for years. She's the best-known bassoonist in all of Scandinavia."

"What do you know about Bitten's personal life?" I asked. "Have you met before?"

"Only once, years ago, when I was still a student. She was playing in Toronto, and I went to see her, and there was a party afterwards. She had a husband then. I guess they're divorced now. I remember her as very encouraging. Other than that, of course, she seemed very old to me. She's probably ten years older than I am."

More like twenty, I thought. "She was much older than Gunther

77

as well. I'd guess she's close to sixty."

"Sixty!"

"Older women can be very attractive," I said primly.

We were approaching the wooden arch of the Accademia Bridge. Perhaps because the *vaporetto's* windows were so fogged up, the arch had a medieval look. The tourists crossing over could have been pilgrims on a religious procession, carrying not cameras, but reliquaries. But Accademia was the stop where Andrew was getting off. I had to find out a little more, and quickly.

"If Bitten didn't kill him, who did?"

Andrew glanced at me. "Well, I must say it doesn't look good for Nicky. I mean, her disappearing like that. I would say she's the most suspicious character, even though I know you're her friend . . . or . . ."

"Friend. And a good one. Because of that, I'm going to let you in on a secret, Andrew, or at least point you in the right direction. If anyone would care to contact the conductor of the Tempus Fugit Ensemble about a concert in Birmingham last night, I think they might get a very good notion of where Nicky was when Gunther met his end."

"Well, that's a relief," said Andrew quickly. "Of course I'll pass on the information to Marco. So she's back in England. I hope you don't think for a minute that I seriously suspected her. It's Anna de Hoog I don't trust," he said, and I could see this new idea taking hold of him. "I felt from the beginning she was taking far too great an interest in poor Gunther. Depressing really, an old girl like that. And she can't play the oboe worth beans."

He got up and began to make for the exit.

"Just one last question, Andrew," I said. "I have some idea why you were following Marco early yesterday morning, but why do you think Marco was following Gunther, especially when it meant leaving Nicky unguarded?"

Andrew shook his handsome boxy head. "All I can imagine is that his father asked him to for some reason. Marco is very tied to his father." The thought did not make him happy, but he shook it off and kissed my cheeks as he left. They were awkward kisses, but well-meant.

I stayed where I was for the approach to San Marco, wondering why he should be so critical of Anna's musical talents when Nicky had said Andrew himself wasn't much of a player. I liked Andrew, even felt some sympathy for him, yet something about him irritated me. Possibly just his being a man. Why should he get a sabbatical and money to research the lives of the women musicians and look for bassoonists at the Pietà, when it was Nicky who really deserved to be able to make her CD-ROM and become famous? I thought back to the moment yesterday when Albert appeared with the bassoon. Andrew said Sandretti had told him the whole story of how the bassoon came to belong to his family, and yet when the instrument turned up, Andrew hadn't appeared to recognize it. Was there a chance he'd stolen the bassoon and let the blame fall on Nicky? Or did I just want to pin a crime on him because he had a huge research grant?

"San Marco!" the conductor shouted, and almost everyone got off except me. I moved to the front of the vaporetto and felt the wind lift the tendrils of hair around my beret. What a day, what a view. Just a week ago I'd dragged in from Sydney, hip and heart smarting from the disastrous expedition with Angela (another academic, damn them all). Now I was chugging alongside the glory of the Palace of the Doges with hardly a care in the world. In spite of Gunther's death, or perhaps because of it.

There is nothing like the shock of a dead body to make you appreciate your own lovely and vigorous life. Especially in Venice.

Nine

IN HIS FORTY-FIFTH YEAR, *weary of literary life, Bashō sold his house and embarked on a journey that he would later describe in* Narrow Road to the Deep North. *It was at this time that he refined his notion that all poetry is based on sabi, a loneliness so profound it becomes no-mind. Along with this sadness comes a certain lightness. One casts off one's personal burdens to better embrace the suffering of the world.*

I too am nearing fifty and tired of the literary world. Like Bashō I am near the end, not of my life, but of the hopeful period of my youth. When I walk down the Peruvian streets where I spent my childhood, it is as if my years of literary success in Japan never happened. I am one with the sorrows of the poor of this South American city.

Sandals torn,
Broken staff.
In Japan, the end of autumn
In Lima, spring.

In spite of my love of afternoons, there is a moment when, unexpectedly, my mood can alter, and the pleasurable melancholy that comes with the lengthening shadows turns to true melancholy. I had motored across the lagoon to the long straight island of the Lido and back again, procrastinating about my book of nuns and ex-nuns on the pampas and enjoying the sight of Venice as it receded into a golden mist and then approached again. I'd disembarked at Arsenale and walked to the small campo in front of the great lions that still guarded the gate to Venice's historic shipyards. There, at a café, I ordered an espresso and glass of water and took out my two novels.

Everything had been perfect; suddenly it became sad as I read *Bashō in Lima*. Loneliness might be no-mind, but it was also lonely. I didn't feel the lightness of casting off my burdens. In fact, I felt burdened as I hadn't earlier, in the golden sunshine, skimming along the surface of the lagoon.

Gunther was dead. As recently as last night he'd been alive and walking not far from here, along the Riva degli Schiavoni. Walking and arguing with Bitten—about something important, if I were to believe Andrew. A quarrel, and he was gone. A chill went through me, and I hastily put away the Bashō book. The shadows were softening into twilight. To stave off the void, I picked up *Lovers and Virgins*; but its unabashed lustiness was not the antidote, and my eyes kept drifting to the four lion statues in front of me as they caught the last rose-blue glow of the sky. Like so many things in Venice, they had been stolen. The two sixth century B.C. lions were taken from Delos. The others were also Greek; one had been part of a fountain long ago. Now the big cats guarded the triumphal arch (beyond which visitors could not go) leading into what had once been the world's greatest naval yard. It had grown with the Crusades; in the sixteenth century fifteen thousand people had worked here. A new ship was launched every day.

By the time Vivaldi was conducting the orchestra in the Pietà, however, at the beginning of the eighteenth century, the power of Venice was waning. It still looked and behaved like a sovereign state, with its doges, ambassadors and spies, its ceremonies and processions. The Arsenale still produced ships, but a growing source of revenue was tourism. Some came for the gambling and the courtesans, some came for the splendor of the music. The production of concertos came to outstrip the production of ships. At the end of the eighteenth century, Napoleon burned the boatyards and sailed away with Venice's remaining fleet. In the dimming light, the Arsenale seemed the very essence of the city's inglorious slide from prosperous, active middle age toward death.

It would break my heart to spend the winter translating *Bashō in Lima*.

I gave up trying to read and paid for my coffee. Perhaps it was time to go back to the hotel, though what I'd do this evening I wasn't sure. I had no lover to dine with; my only friend in Venice was determinedly reclusive for the moment. All the same, I couldn't leave Venice yet. I was relieved Nicky had had no part in Gunther's demise, but there was no saying what mischief she might still get up to.

Strolling back toward the Riva along the short stretch of canal, I saw a red-haired slip of a girl in a white shirt with a tall collar jump off the *vaporetto* and dash into the naval museum. Without quite thinking it through, I crossed over the bridge and went into the museum too.

The Museo Storico Navale was much bigger than I'd suspected: four floors of gondolas and other marine vessels and equipment. I cursed my hip as I slowly climbed the stairs and wandered through the exhibits. I had always imagined, when I heard the story of the

Doge performing the ceremony of Venice's marriage to the sea, that the ring he threw into the Adriatic was a gold band off his own finger. But here, in a glass case, I saw rings the size of salad plates, rings the size of big glazed donuts, hollow inside, encrusted with jewels. A card in the case said the ring was attached to a long cord, so that after it was tossed into the sea, it could be retrieved. That seemed like cheating on the marriage vows to me. On another floor was a model of the last gold-encrusted *Bucintoro*, the ceremonial ship that the Doge, in golden cap and crimson, ermine-trimmed gown, had used when he went to the sea to pronounce, "We marry you, oh sea, in token of our true and perpetual dominion."

There was no sign of Francesca, and I wondered if I'd dreamed up her presence out of my own loneliness. Hardly anyone was in the vast museum at all. It was near closing time, and I suspected this was a museum most visitors never managed to get to, wonderful as it was with its models of fighting galleys, its full-size gondolas black as ravens, its figureheads. One figurehead represented Venice as a woman in a low-necked dress, dangling scales in one hand and accompanied by a lion. The scales looked tilted.

I sat down on a wide wooden bench next to a gondola on display, and took out the two Latin American books, yet again (at least Simon could never accuse me of not *trying* to come to terms with this literature). I had a strong compulsion to hide *Lovers and Virgins* in the gondola, to remove myself from its pernicious influence, but I simply placed it to one side and opened *Bashō in Lima*. I couldn't help thinking that when a woman renounced the world, as this narrator suggested she wanted to do, it meant something very different than when a man did. It was clearly in the interests of men that we renounce worldly goods and desires. Then they could have more for themselves. To want too much—to want anything—was the way to heartbreak and suffering. Yet for centuries women had lived such circumscribed lives. How could we ever know what too much was?

"Cassandra!" said Francesca, coming around the corner with her arm linked in Roberta's.

"You're here too?" asked Roberta in a less than welcoming manner.

It was the first time I'd seen them since the events of last night. We all must have thought of that horrible moment on the bridge, because for a moment there was silence. I considered again how much Roberta looked like her brother. They were both very handsome. I wondered if Roberta and Francesca met at the museum regularly. It was certainly deserted enough for a tête-à-tête between two women who might have nowhere else to go.

With an attempt at cheerfulness, I said, "I've always wanted to see this museum. You can't really get a good notion of a gondola just by looking at them swarming around the Grand Canal, can you? You pretty much need to see the keel to get the true picture . . . I had no idea that I'd run into you and Francesca here. I'm delighted. And Roberta, I'm especially pleased to see you because I have some questions to ask you. A friend of mine is preparing a CD-ROM on women musicians of Vivaldi's time, and she hopes to speak with you and get your assistance since you're another musician, a very accomplished one, I might add."

"Which friend?" Roberta asked, but she looked a little less irritated than she had when she first saw me.

"Nicola Gibbons."

"The one who stole my family's bassoon?"

"She didn't steal it, and anyway, it's been found. Sort of."

"I'm not an expert, but I can speak with your friend. We can meet tomorrow. Give me her phone number. I'll call her."

The two of them seemed to be moving off. I supposed, because of Francesca's work and her mother, they didn't have much time together. Still I was reluctant to be left alone quite yet. "She doesn't have a phone . . . She's so busy at the moment that she asked me to do some research for her, you know, just ask the initial questions, make the arrangements for interviews . . ."

"What questions?" Roberta asked.

"Tell me, just for a start, about the musicians at the Pietà. It sounds like a golden age." I patted the bench next to me, but they remained standing.

"It was no golden age for the women in the Pietà," Roberta said. "Of course compared to some of the other options, like being a servant or prostitute, being raised to make music in a protected environment meant you had some degree of freedom within that limited sphere. But it was difficult to leave one of the *ospedali* without getting married, and even if you managed to marry a sympathetic man, you often had to sign an agreement that you would not perform in public or carry on with a musical career. Very few women managed to get out of the Pietà and find work as musicians. A few became singers. So you can see why women committed to music simply stayed at the *ospedali*."

"Nicky finds it fascinating that Vivaldi composed so many bassoon concertos. She wonders if there was a very talented bassoonist at the Pietà."

"Yes, possibly, but it may also be that the bassoon was just an instrument that drew out some of his best work, his deepest feelings. The cello and the bassoon have some similarities, you know. They both have deep registers and can create a very rich, melancholy sound. And then, you know, Vivaldi loved conversation among instruments, and the bassoon is capable of having a dialogue with itself. You can get high notes as well as low notes, back and forth, just like people talking."

"Do you think there were other composers, women, who wrote for the bassoon?"

"There were certainly women composers in all the *ospedali*. Much of the library of the Pietà still exists, but no one has ever completely cataloged it. Some of that library might be at the Conservatory of Music. I have a friend, Giovanna, who teaches there who might be able to help." Roberta looked at me impatiently. "But if your friend Nicky is a bassoon scholar like the rest of them, I'm sure she knows far more than I."

Francesca seemed thoughtful. "I heard several people last night at the bridge asking where Nicky was."

"She had to fly to Birmingham to perform in a concert," I said quickly. "She returned this morning, but she's not staying with Signore Sandretti any longer. She said—she doesn't trust him."

Roberta nodded.

"She's really wild to get this CD-ROM project off the ground. Everything that's happened—the theft of the bassoon, Gunther's murder—has been an impediment." Now I was talking like the single-minded Nicky herself. "I don't mean that Gunther's death was an obstacle. It was terribly sad—and mysterious."

Francesca was pulling at Roberta's arm. "Arrange something with Giovanna," she said.

"All right. We'll meet tomorrow, you, me and Nicky—if she can—at the Conservatory of Music, during my lunch break, at one o'clock. We'll see what we can find in the library."

"*Ciao,*" said Francesca, giving me a little wave as Roberta pulled her off.

Before you could nobly renounce something or someone you had to have it to begin with.

I took the *vaporetto* back over to the Dorsoduro. The evening air was soft and all around me I heard Italian. It was the hour when the day-trippers had left and other tourists were perhaps resting at their hotels before venturing out again to restaurants. After my encounter with Roberta and Francesca, I had a reason to hunt up Nicky. I'd drag her out to dinner and tell her about the research date tomorrow at the conservatory. But when I alighted at Accademia, I encountered Anna de Hoog almost immediately. She was standing in front of a rack of postcards in the little square in front of the museum and looking more secretive than ever, but also a bit wild-eyed.

"What's up?" I asked.

"Frigga has arrived at the *palazzo*."

"Gunther's girlfriend!"

"No," Anna said. "Frigga is his grandmother, as it turns out. Frau Frigga Hausen."

She tried to seem surprised by that, but I didn't buy it. I was also curious why she seemed to be hovering, coatless and purseless, by the *vaporetto* stop. There was about her something of precipitous flight. Or was she waiting for someone?

"Why don't you stop off at the *palazzo*?" suggested Anna.

"I have no desire to meet Frigga."

"I wasn't thinking of her so much as Bitten."

"What about Bitten?" I was a little startled. Anna could not possibly know that Bitten claimed to be Olivia's granddaughter.

"Bitten and Frigga have been quarreling. Bitten says she and Gunther planned to get married in Stockholm this week. Frigga says that's nonsense: the two of them only met five or six days ago. Bitten is in a—how shall I say it?—vulnerable state of mind. She might need a drink. If you suggested it. Ah, here's the *vaporetto*."

I didn't think Anna had rushed out of the *palazzo* with the intention of taking a *vaporetto* anywhere. But as she blended in with the crowd surging onto the boat, I realized Anna had given me the impetus I needed to do a little sleuthing on Nicky's behalf. I was less interested in who had killed Gunther than in stopping Bitten from destroying Nicky's life. It had not yet occurred to me to wonder if the two things were in any way related.

But it had occurred to me that if Bitten did manage to establish a claim on Olivia's property and wrest the London house away from Nicky, that I too would have no place to live. Like Bashō after his home burned down, I'd be out on my ear.

Ten

FRIGGA WAS NOT what I expected. I'd imagined one of those sleek German girls, blond, buxom, thin, with a dark indoor tan, who was just beginning to thicken around the middle from years of cream-laden tortes. Even when Anna had said that Frigga was Gunther's grandmother, I had merely done a little mental rearranging and added fifty pounds instead of ten.

But Frigga was old, eighty at least, with wrinkled, spotted skin and red-rimmed dark eyes. She was wearing a smart pink Chanel suit from the 1950s, with a black shawl over her shoulders, heavy support stockings and well-polished orthopedic shoes. When I arrived, she was sitting in the garden speaking in stilted English to Marco. There was no sign of Andrew, or of Bitten, but from upstairs came the mournful adagio Bitten had played this morning.

"I will not leave Venice until I find out who murdered him."

From the expression on Marco's face, I had a feeling that Frigga had said this more than once.

"Ah, Cassandra," he said. "This is the grandmother of Gunther,

Frau Hausen. We have been to the police station, and we have heard the results. Gunther died of water in the lungs, very sad. To date the police have no witnesses and no motives. So perhaps Gunther only had a misstep, they think."

"I know he was killed," said Frigga. "I begged him to be careful, always to take special precautions with his stomach when he traveled and not drink too much coffee. I tried to protect him, his whole life, just like I tried to protect his family. I failed. They all are dead. All dead. And I live on and on. I don't understand."

I didn't really understand either. Gunther hardly seemed like the type to have enemies. Unless of course he'd been a drug courier or had a criminal past. But as far as I knew from his biography in the program, and from what Nicky said, Gunther had been playing and teaching the Baroque bassoon for the past ten years in Düsseldorf.

"I will not leave Venice until I find out who murdered him," she said again, and Marco's eyes glazed over. With an effort he said, "We go out to dinner now, yes? To the local restaurant with many Venetian specialty dishes. Have you ever had squid in its own ink, Mrs. Hausen? You will like to come too, Mrs. Reilly?"

In spite of my sympathy for Marco, I couldn't think of many worse ways to spend the evening.

"I have a tremendous amount of work to do. But I'm sure Andrew would love to join you. Meanwhile, I'll just have a quick word with Bitten." I went into the *palazzo*.

It was difficult to believe that when I'd first met Bitten a few days ago, she'd seemed a lusty Swede, in ripe middle age, bursting out of her silk shirt. Now her skin was no longer soft and plump; she was like a slice of orange that had been left out overnight. She'd put her bassoon to the side and was sitting in a corner of the room with a glass of wine. I asked her if she'd like some dinner. She shrugged and gestured to me to sit down on the bed. I could see there were two suitcases in the room and wondered if one of them was Gunther's.

"Did you know Frigga was Gunther's grandmother?" I began, not exactly where I'd planned.

"She calls herself his grandmother, but she's really his great-grandmother," Bitten said. "Gunther's mother was her granddaughter; she took her in as a baby and raised her. Gunther's mother died when he was a child, and Frigga took him in."

"That's a sad story," I said.

"Gunther's was the third violent death in three generations. Unbelievable," said Bitten, rubbing her forearms. "If anyone, you would have thought Gunther could have broken the spell. He had the spirit of an angel."

"Do you think he was murdered then?"

"I don't know."

"You said violent death."

"No one goes into a canal easily. Unless they commit suicide. But why would he do that? He had everything to look forward to. We had everything to look forward to."

In the face of her obvious grief, I felt unsure how to continue. This didn't seem like quite the right time to ask her about the quarrel Marco and Andrew had overheard her having with Gunther the night he died. Nor did I feel quite right grilling her on a few other aspects of the case, such as why she'd always seemed so put out when Gunther got a phone call from Frigga. I didn't want to appear unsympathetic and lose her. My only recourse was to keep up the concerned front and press on, even though it made me feel a bit of a fraud. "You haven't had such an easy time of it yourself, I imagine," I said.

No, she hadn't! Under the influence of another glass of wine, she told me about her unhappy marriage to and divorce from a man who hadn't really supported her. If he had, who knows what heights she might have reached with an international recording career. Instead she had often chosen to stay close to home and to teach and perform mainly in Sweden. And in the end it hadn't helped, because Sven left her anyway . . . after twenty years.

An unhappy Marco came to the door and announced he was taking Frigga to dinner. He had seen no sign of Andrew. Would we consider joining them? Poor Marco! As soon as he was gone, Bitten opened up another bottle of wine. This time she poured me a glass too.

"So much death!" she sighed. "My mother died only a month ago. And my grandmother six months ago."

"I'm sorry."

"The worst of it is, I never knew my grandmother. How much I would have liked to have known her! She was a famous musician, you see. Olivia Wulf."

"Your grandmother was Olivia Wulf?"

"Yes." Bitten went to a bureau and pulled out a photograph. It was Olivia with a young man and woman. I realized I'd seen the same photograph in Olivia's study.

"This is my mother and father and grandmother." Bitten paused. "How well do you know Nicola?"

"How well do any of us know each other?" I said soulfully and raised my glass.

We toasted, but then Bitten looked confused. "She called you to help her."

"Only because I happened to know a man here who knows a bit about stolen art objects."

"Ah, yes. Albert." I could see Bitten's now well-lubricated mind sailing off in the uneasy direction of Albert Egmont and the mystery of the stolen bassoon that had not been accepted as the stolen bassoon by Signore Sandretti.

I said quickly, "It must have made Nicky so happy when she found out that you were Olivia's granddaughter. You know that she lived with Olivia for years."

"Happy!" Bitten banged the coffee table with a large foot. "No, Nicola was not happy. Because *she* had been imagining that Olivia was her grandmother and that she deserved everything that Olivia had."

"Did you just tell her recently?"

"Yes. Here, the second day. We had a very bad quarrel. A pity because I had hoped to be friends."

"How did you find out about Olivia?"

"I was visiting my mother in the nursing home six months ago, when she stared at me and stared at the newspaper she was reading and said, mysteriously, 'I wonder if it's true that musical talent runs in the family.'

"I thought it was a case of my mother's mind wandering, especially when I looked at the newspaper later and saw that my mother had been reading the obituary of Olivia Wulf, a musician I had only heard of slightly. But last month, after my mother died, I was going through her things and discovered an old scrapbook of photographs that showed my mother as a young woman, with a young man and a woman who seemed to be his mother. Underneath was written, *me with Jakob and Olivia Wulf, Vienna, 1936.* This is the photograph.

"I knew my mother was Austrian, of course, but she always said she had come to Sweden with her mother during the war. She said she'd met my father, Carl Johansson, at university. My father had died years before, but I found an elderly relative of his who said that, yes, she thought that my mother, Elizabeth, had been married before. When I asked if it was possible I could have been the child of her first husband and not Carl's, the relative said she couldn't recall anything about the circumstances of my birth, not even if I'd been born before or after my mother and Carl were married. She said, 'During the war, everything was so confused. Everyone got mixed up about who they were and what they were doing.'

"On the one hand I was shocked, because this news meant I could be older than I'd thought, and that seemed impossible. I have no memories of war or of a flight to Sweden, only of growing up in a peaceful suburb outside Stockholm. But I decided to find out more about Olivia Wulf, and that's when I came across the information that Olivia's son was called Jakob. I found my mother's entry papers to Sweden from 1940, and discovered she had arrived as a refugee. There was no mention of Jakob entering. She was never a student at the university, though my father was. My own birth certificate is from 1943, but when I went back to the hospital where I had supposedly been born, they had no record of my mother ever having been a patient. They said that wasn't unusual, to lose records from those years, but it still struck me as strange."

"But if Elizabeth survived the war and got to Sweden with you, why didn't she contact Olivia through the Red Cross? Why didn't she tell Olivia she had a granddaughter?"

"My mother would never talk about the war. Whatever happened to Jakob must have been horrible. Now when I look back I remember how she would cry whenever there was a documentary about the Holocaust. My father, Carl, forbade me ever to ask her questions because of what she had been through."

"What are you going to do now?" I asked.

"I'm going to claim my rightful inheritance," Bitten said, lying down on the bed and kicking off her shoes. She looked tired, but her voice was firm, if a little slurred from drink. "I'm going to claim everything that's mine."

I left Bitten reclining on her bed. No one else seemed to be in the house. It was curious that Andrew was still out. Perhaps he was waiting until Frigga was safely back in her hotel before he pounced on Marco again. I thought I might as well take a look through the room Nicky had been staying in when I arrived. No one was there. I had just pulled the mattress up when Anna de Hoog entered quietly.

"Are you searching for something?"

It was fairly useless to deny that I was, and yet I stalled, dropping the upper mattress and sitting heavily down on it. Taking a hint from Bitten, I mumbled in a slurred voice, "The Swede and I had a few too many glasses of wine, I guess. Wasn't sure I could manage to get back to my hotel. Thought about Nicky's room next door all free and clear. Why not sleep here, I thought. Just checking around for a little of the duty-free."

Anna laughed. "Let me get my bottle of brandy." She went out.

Dear Mother of Christ. Was she going to get me drunk? I had let Bitten do almost all the drinking earlier, but I wasn't sure Anna would let me get away with that.

When she returned Anna was wearing a kimono and slippers. She poured me a glass of brandy and watched as I sipped it. She took a hearty slug.

"So, was Bitten able to tell you anything you didn't know?"

"I don't know what your interest in these people is," I said. "You're an oboist—at least you claim you are—and they're bassoonists. Who invited you to this conference anyway? Signore Sandretti? You seem to be pretty tight with him." I remembered the two of them arriving together when Albert was showing us the missing bassoon. More important, Sandretti had been one of the first people at the scene of the discovery of Gunther's body, appearing at the Danieli shortly after Anna herself.

"Signore Sandretti did invite me to the conference, as a matter of fact. He invited everyone."

The brandy was doing its work, on top of the two glasses of wine with Bitten. I hadn't had dinner either. I noticed my body was assuming a slightly more prone position than I'd intended.

"But he didn't invite you because of your musical skills, I bet."

Anna laughed. She was certainly more attractive when she laughed than when she played the oboe. "Let's say I'm here in a special capacity. To keep an eye on some things."

"You didn't keep an eye on the bassoon."

"The way the bassoon went missing came as a surprise," she allowed.

I took a leap in the dark, a mental leap that is, because my body was getting more and more relaxed. "You were supposed to be watching Gunther, I bet. That's why Frigga is so convinced he died from foul play. He was involved in something illegal, wasn't he?"

"I have no evidence Gunther was involved in anything illegal," Anna said, but I wasn't sure I believed her. She moved closer to pour me another drink, and this time she stayed seated on the bed. As she leaned over to fill my glass, the neck of her kimono swung open, revealing a high firm breast.

I muttered something about virgins, I believe, and renunciation versus passion. I think I may have spoken of the need for pilgrimage. I know I protested slightly when my clothes began to come off; I tried again to voice my suspicions that Anna was working for somebody, if not Sandretti, then perhaps Frigga herself. She had definitely been avoiding Frigga. My thought process, however, grew more and more muddled, and in the end the only admission I was able to draw out of Anna was that, no, the oboe was not her first instrument; she had actually studied the trombone and that was some years ago.

I woke up in the morning, surprisingly naked under the sheets. I had a headache and at first only a hazy memory of the past evening's events. It took Marco's shocked face at the door to alert me to the possibility that something had gone awry with my sleuthing. The biography of the well-known conductor that I'd brought from Nicky's house in London lay by my head on the pillow, with a brief note: "This is possibly what you were looking for. Regards, Anna de Hoog."

Eleven

SHEEPISHLY, THOUGH WITH LESS guilt than one would expect, I let myself out of the *palazzo* and found a café, where I had a bracing cappuccino and a croissant. When my head was a little clearer, I began to seriously page through the biography. It was inscribed to Olivia in memory of "all we went through during the war." Midway through the book it became obvious that the author had been Olivia's lover, the conductor who had arranged for her to get out of Vienna and to England.

"Unfortunately," he wrote, "Olivia's son, Jakob, was not able to come with us that day. He promised to join us very soon. Olivia believed it was his fiancée Elizabeth who held him back. She was not Jewish and did not see the danger in the way we did. Like millions of others, Jakob and Elizabeth were swallowed up in the horrors that followed. Jakob was picked up by the Nazis. Elizabeth vanished. It was a great tragedy in Olivia's life that she was never able to save her son. She made several trips to the Continent after the war and eventually learned he had died at Dachau of pneumonia. A survivor of the camp remembered that Jakob had spoken of a wife and daughter, but Olivia found no trace of a child."

Nicky had never mentioned to me that Olivia suspected her son and his wife had had a daughter, and that she'd searched for them. But Nicky must have known, and asked me to bring the biography to confirm her memory. No wonder she was so upset when Bitten turned up claiming to be Olivia's granddaughter. It had to be true. Jakob had died at Dachau, and Elizabeth had escaped to Sweden with her young daughter in 1940 and remarried. Of course, Bitten didn't seem to remember anything of her early years; everyone knew now that survivors of great trauma often blocked out memories that were too painful.

If Bitten *was* Olivia's granddaughter, and it seemed quite likely she was, no wonder Nicky was nervous.

Nicky! I looked at my watch. The meeting with Roberta and her friend Giovanna was scheduled for one at the conservatory, and it was now ten thirty. I had to find Nicky's hotel and let her know. "Yes, I'm sure I can find it," I had said to her yesterday, waving away her offer of a hand-drawn map. "The Frari, of course. You can't miss the Frari," I'd said, forgetting that in Venice even a huge church like Santa Maria Gloriosa dei Frari could disappear into the closely-packed buildings around it.

I went around in circles for half an hour until I found the tiny hotel in the "alley near the Frari" almost by accident. Bassoon music wafted from an upper story. At the reception desk, the clerk looked blank when I asked for Signora Gibbons in room seven. "No one of that name is here." Were those her instructions, or was she passing herself off as someone else? She must be here; I could hear the bassoon.

Of course. She was using my passport. I slapped my forehead and apologized to the clerk. "She must be using her married name.

Signora Reilly, is that how she registered?"

He nodded and then said shyly, "Are you her sister? You look like her picture in the passport."

"No I'm not her sister!" I said, and then coughed. "Actually—she's my cousin."

I went upstairs and heard the bassoon behind the door. "I know you're in there, Nicky," I said. "Open up."

Reluctantly she dragged herself to the door. She was wearing a large T-shirt that said VENEZIA, which she must have bought at the airport, and velvet stretch pants.

"Come on," I said briskly. "I have news of various sorts, but I can tell you on the way to the Conservatory of Music. We're going to do a little research."

"Thanks, but no," she said, picking up her bassoon again. "I've just come to a place of great satisfaction and joy in my rehearsing, and I plan to stay with that for the morning. Later maybe."

"But I thought you wanted to know more about the girls in the Pietà."

Ignoring me completely, she plunged into a long and eerie passage. "Who do you think that is?"

"Shostakovich?"

"No, it's Vivaldi. It's amazing; there are times when I think I've completely pegged him, that I know him and his way of writing for the bassoon inside and out. The cheeriness, the chattiness, his way of making the bassoon carry the weight of the world for a few long bars, only to resolve it in a laugh. Then, all of a sudden, I'll be completely taken aback by how modern he sounds. What he could *do* with the bassoon—not just the usual sounds. You know, Cassandra, a lot of people have captured the bassoon's *longing,* and that sort of stockinged-feet-tiptoeing-into-a-room sound. And, of course, *everybody* always makes it the buffoon of the orchestra. When the symphony composer wants a clumsy, stumbling bumpkin, he always writes in the bassoon. Like this—"

Nicky jumped up and advanced on me, humming some bars from *Peter and the Wolf*. Her auburn curls flew wildly. I backed off. Clearly she had been spending far too much time alone with this instrument. She waved her hands about. "But Vivaldi doesn't caricature the bassoon; he doesn't make the bassoon a buffoon. He'll do fussy, he'll do bickering, but purely comic squabbling—never. You get the dialogue, you get spirited conversation. You get laughing, you get sighing. I know all that. And then suddenly, I'm playing a passage and realize, the next composer to create this eeriness is Sibelius."

Nicky plumped down on her bed, completely overjoyed. "He's a genius. You just can't come to the end of Vivaldi. Though I wonder," she said, lying back on the pillows, lifting her leg in the air and regarding her ankle, "if he didn't get a teeny touch of inspiration from Monteverdi's *Orfeo*. The bassoon is prominent in the passages in the underworld. There's some eeriness there, definitely."

"I thought you wanted to meet Roberta," I said impatiently.

"Roberta who?"

"Roberta Sandretti. Marco's sister, the clarinetist. I've gone to a lot of trouble to arrange this visit to the library. Her friend Giovanna, who teaches the violin, is going to help us."

"Cassandra, why didn't you say so to begin with? *Of course* I want to come."

She jumped up and began gathering her things and thrusting her feet into a ridiculous pair of pumps.

"We don't have to be there for an hour and a half," I said. "No need to pinch your toes longer than necessary. We can go have a bite and then stroll over in a leisurely way."

"I don't have time for lunch."

"Why not?"

"You don't think I can wear this T-shirt to meet Roberta Sandretti, do you? To do research in a library? I've got to go shopping."

I pounded down the stairs behind her. "Just don't be late," I said, as she vanished out the door.

The desk clerk looked admiringly after her. "Your cousin is very vigorous," he said. "I hear her playing the *fagotto*. She has very good lungs." He gestured approvingly to his chest and stared in a disappointed way at my own.

"She's a famous *fagotto* player," I said. "It's meant to build you up." Which reminded me: Where was Albert with that old *fagotto* anyway? I hadn't seen him all yesterday. I hadn't seen him since after the concert. I still had some time to kill before one. I decided to take the *vaporetto* over to the Riva degli Schiavoni and see if I could locate Albert at the Hotel Danieli.

The Danieli was the sort of hotel that made me feel that any moment after my tentative, soft-shoed entry, a security man might grab my elbows and escort me forcibly out. Fanciful glass chandeliers swung from the high gilt ceiling. Marble stairs zigzagged upwards in a dazzling painterly perspective. Bellhops hefted sleek suitcases, followed by skeleton-thin women in tiny black suits. In the lobby, elegant men sat in leather chairs, smoking and leafing through *La Stampa* and *The Times*. In vain I told myself that George Sand, Ruskin, Wagner and Proust had stayed here and that if I wore dark glasses and assumed a haughty British accent, I'd fit right in.

I didn't of course. Receptionists can always tell. The uniformed desk clerk had narrow shoulders, hollow cheeks and little black eyes that could probably show obsequiousness, but not to the likes of me.

"Albert Egmont? No, I'm sorry he is not a guest at the hotel."

He dismissed me quickly, with a haughty British accent of his own, implying that it would be very peculiar indeed should I know a guest at the Danieli.

"I don't understand. Has he checked out?"

With a show of taking great and unnecessary pains, the clerk flipped back a page or two. "I don't see that this person was ever a guest here."

"But I . . ." He turned away, more obviously rude now, to speak to a guest, a woman with a fur hat sitting on her head like a party of dead squirrels. She had an Argentinean accent.

There was nothing to do but take my Joan Plowright imitation and leave. But suddenly I found one of the porters giving me a wink and a surreptitious gesture that said to follow him down a short hall. Well! This hadn't happened to me in many years. I didn't know whether to laugh or be annoyed. Then I noticed he seemed to be mouthing the name "Albert." I went after him and turned into a small room filled with left luggage.

"Please, you speak Italian?"

"Yes."

"Your friend Alberto is my friend also," he said. "You wish to find him?"

"Actually, yes. Him and his bassoon."

"He is not a guest here at the hotel. He is staying elsewhere. At a hotel near the train station. It was an old monastery once. I have forgotten its name, but if you ask near the station, they will know it." Hearing the ring of the desk bell, he started to leave, but I stopped him. I'd noticed with a shock that we were almost next to the glass door leading to the dock and the canal.

"Wait," I said. "Were you here the night the German man was found in the water?"

"Yes, but I was here, in the left luggage, not on the dock. It was the doorman who found the body."

"Then you were here when Signore Alberto came earlier that evening to drop off the bassoon in the left luggage." I cast my eyes quickly around for a paper-wrapped parcel resembling a long frankfurter.

The desk bell gave an irritated ping-ping. "He left no parcel."

"If Alberto is keeping such a low profile, why are you letting me know where he is? Other people are looking for him. The police, for instance. Are you telling the police where he is? If not, then why me?"

"He said if a woman, a very *lovely*, tall woman with a beret from the Canadian Army, comes to ask for him, I must tell her where to find him."

I was sure Albert had not said *lovely*. But the porter had whisked off.

I took the opportunity to sneak out onto the dock and look around. The canal was busy, as usual. Timing was everything in whatever had happened. Except for the ten minutes he was gone to deposit the bassoon—when Gunther was firmly before my eyes—Albert was with me at the Pietà through all of *Orlando Furioso*. Marco and Andrew were gone for the third act but were presumably together. Bitten's movements were unaccounted for, except that she'd left the Pietà with Gunther during the middle of Act Two. Anna of course had been playing, though there might have been enough time during the intermission to kill Gunther. Signore Sandretti? He'd made an appearance before the performance and another at the end, but where had he been in the middle? And Albert had certainly said something about the Danieli to Marco before the performance began. Had they agreed to meet? Had Albert left the bassoon here? And when had he taken it away? Or had he been the one to pick it up again?

I took a good look at the canal. Gunther could have been pushed from any number of places. From this dock, from the bridge, or from the pavement on the other side of the canal where the water surged up. That would have been the darkest place. Of course, Gunther could have been pushed in from someplace farther up the canal, perhaps from one of those dead-end narrow alleys. Even a window was possible.

"Is Madame still here?" the front desk receptionist, he of the narrow shoulders and beady black eyes asked, suddenly appearing behind me. "Are you still looking for your . . . friend?"

In another moment he'd be having me searched to see if I had one of the chandeliers tucked into my leather bomber jacket.

"I'm hoping to find a water taxi, my good man," I said, now Queen Victoria as played by Judi Dench.

The desk clerk snapped his fingers, and a water taxi appeared from nowhere.

"The Conservatory of Music," I said grandly. I held out a folded note, a large note, but as the receptionist reached for it, I managed to drop it into the water. In spite of himself, he scrambled for it, and that was a sight I wouldn't have missed.

The water taxi headed out toward the Grand Canal. It was madness to spend Nicky's money this way. Dropping thousands of *lire* into the canal to make a silly point; dropping thousands more on a trip through the most touristy, gondola-clogged stretch of water in Venice. Was I losing my mind? Still, the Church of Santa Maria della Salute, with its huge snails of Baroque buttresses guarding or glorifying the entrance into the Grand Canal was one of the world's great sights. It was best seen from the water, I told myself. Might as well enjoy it. It was, after all, *Nicky's* money.

A hundred steps beyond the Salute, I'd be in the depths of the Dorsoduro, back into the city's dense orchestration of stone: dark corners, leaning towers, street mazes to leave you reeling. Venice could feel heavy and concentrated, with only brief snatches of sky and sky reflected in the narrow canals. Out here on the water, however, density was left behind for something far more transparent and insubstantial. The heaviest villas and palaces wavered in the sunlight; their watery reflections were even less solid.

Walls of stone
Under water
Break into clouds.

I definitely felt a mood of *sabi* coming on. I reached into my satchel for *Bashō in Lima*, but came up with *Lovers and Virgins* instead. I stared at the cover—not at the plunging necklines and nuns' habits of the illustration, but at the scribbles I'd made when Nicky had called me from Venice. Nicky's money. Nicky's money.

I remembered Albert looking with interest at the book, the wet morning I'd run into him in the Piazza San Marco. The bassoon articles meant nothing to him; neither could the conductor's biography. Then I realized that next to the word *safe*, I'd scrawled *combination in lentils*.

It wouldn't take a genius to figure out the meaning of that note. All it would take is someone who knew my address in London, who knew that both Nicky and I were here in Venice, and who was perhaps not as honest as he could be.

Twelve

THE CONSERVATORY OF MUSIC was housed in a sprawling old *palazzo* off Campo San Stefano. Once white, the enormous building was now stained with the soot of pollution and rain. The exterior was studded barbarically with blackened heads, but there was an undeniable, though broken-down grandeur to the place. A vast, ghostly courtyard of colonnades, bounded at one end by mesh netting full of pigeon feathers, added to the derelict effect. A great Venetian family had lived where now a few hundred students studied. From the upper stories came piano chords and snatches of saxophone and trumpet.

I hadn't expected Nicky to be on time and was a little late myself, yet there she was, in a corner of the square in front of the conservatory, attempting to blend into the base of a statue. She was dressed, unusually for her, in a sober suit of gray with a long skirt. She'd purchased sensible oxfords and had managed to twist her auburn curls up into a knot. This must be her notion of what a researcher might wear. She even had glasses on a chain around her neck and an elegant leather briefcase.

Boyish in jeans and running shoes, Roberta was lounging impatiently at the peeling front door. "Quick," she said, after shaking hands with Nicky. "The chief librarian is at lunch. My friend Giovanna is going to take us up. Otherwise they never let anyone into the library."

"Why, are the materials so precious?" I asked.

"No, they are too lazy," she said.

The interior of the building was as grand as the outside. We went up a massive staircase to the *piano nobile*, its floor inlaid with pink and gray marble. It was empty save for some large Rococo paintings and a few gilt chairs, and a number of doors. In that, it was like the Sandrettis' home, but on a much grander scale. All the rooms led off from the *piano nobile*, giving a fairy-tale sense of choice: Which door led to the sacks of gold and which to the dungeon? Which to the tiger and which to the woman? We opened one door and found ourselves in the library, which, especially in comparison to the grand empty hall outside, was small and cramped. A young man was paging through librettos and making copies at a photocopier. A woman with green-rimmed round glasses and an inch of strawberry-pink hair was flipping through the *New Grove Dictionary of Women Composers* in front of her on a long wooden table. Her short sleeveless dress was strawberry to match her hair.

"Giovanna," Roberta said in English for Nicky's benefit, "is a teacher of the violin here. She knows a great deal about the Baroque era."

Giovanna looked more like a ladybug than a music professor, but she had a winning smile and serious eyes.

"Shall we?" Giovanna said, and without another word the four of us disappeared into a back room filled with shelves and files.

"Are these Vivaldi manuscripts?" I asked, as Giovanna began to pull out boxes full of scores. She set the boxes on a table, took off the large glasses and replaced them with a smaller pair of reading specs. She did everything very precisely. She had very beautiful long fingers. I noticed that Nicky was uncharacteristically silent.

"It's unlikely. Almost everything of Vivaldi's, his original scores, is in a library in Turin," Giovanna said. "There were many bound volumes found in a monastery in the 1920s. Before that, if you can believe it, Vivaldi had been almost unknown for over two hundred years. People knew his name, but he was considered a very minor musician. But when they found all his manuscripts and began to catalog and play them, they discovered just what a genius he was."

"And now we hear Vivaldi's *Four Seasons* all four seasons of the year until we are sick to death of him," said Roberta. "It is a terrible irony, isn't it, to go from obscurity to superfluity in just a few decades."

Giovanna smiled. She had pretty lips, also strawberry colored. "Some of us are not as enchanted by the Baroque as others."

"If you worked in a classical music shop, you would feel the same about Vivaldi," said Roberta. "What about Galuppi, what about Marcello, what about Monteverdi, I ask the tourists. What about Barbara Strozzi? For that matter, what about Philip Glass and Arvo Pärt? But no, the tourists are in Venice. They want *The Four Seasons*."

Giovanna opened up several of the boxes. "These were probably scores of the Pietà musicians. It's unlikely any would be in Vivaldi's own hand, despite his having composed them for the Pietà. He would have worked with copyists to break down the orchestration in parts, so you would have five violin scores, for instance. Life before the copy machine." She riffled through the scores. "There is some arrangement to this, but we'd have to investigate. I'm not a research specialist, unfortunately, and you would have to have several letters of recommendation and so on for the chief librarian to let you spread everything out and really look at it for days on end. I'm sure, with your reputation," she smiled at Nicky, "we could easily arrange that."

Still Nicky was silent. She stared around her at the stacks and shelves of boxes. She looked, with a very dissatisfied expression, at her neatly tied, clunky oxfords.

"What exactly are you searching for?" Roberta prodded.

"Roberta told me you want to make a CD-ROM collection of Vivaldi's bassoon concertos," said Giovanna.

Nicky seemed to wake up. "Original bassoon music by a woman composer who might have lived and worked at the Pietà, that's what I'm looking for."

"I see the idea has expanded," I said. "With Nicky, ideas often do."

Nicky opened her new leather briefcase. "I want," she said impressively, "to put the Pietà on the map again." She took out a sort of prospectus from a folder of marbled paper. There was her CV, an overview of the CD-ROM project, a list of bassoon concertos to be performed on compact disc, and color reproductions of the interior of the Pietà church. She handed it all to Giovanna.

"Originally," Nicky said, "I imagined the project to be completely about Vivaldi, with women musicians performing his work. But now the concept is changing. If it's possible—I know it must be possible—I want to find music composed by one of the orphaned bassoonists. I want to find out about her. I want to weave her story through the CD-ROM project. Perhaps a video documentary. Maybe something for the BBC. A co-production with Italian television."

"I love the idea," said Giovanna. "But—it may be difficult to find such music. "Would this bassoon composer have signed her compositions? Probably not. The women of the *cori* were not encouraged to think of themselves as anything other than members of the orchestra or as teachers." She pulled out a large leather-bound volume with scores bound in, and the name *Anna Maria* stamped in gold on the cover. "Here is an exception. Anna Maria was a *maestra*, probably around 1720, at the Pietà. She was well known for her proficiency on the harpsichord, cello, lute, mandolin and, of course, violin. She was one of Vivaldi's brightest stars."

Giovanna opened the leather book. "Here you see the scores for the first violin of many of Vivaldi's concerti. But they are Vivaldi's works. As far as is known, Anna Maria composed nothing herself."

"Or so they would like us to believe," said Roberta. "It's very irritating. All those women musicians—some of them *must* have composed something!"

"You know about Maddalena Lombardini Sirmen?" Giovanna asked Nicky.

"Of course."

"She was in the *cori* of the Mendicanti," Giovanna explained to me. "Another of the *ospedali*. She was a well-known violinist, and around 1770 she was able to leave her *ospedale* to marry the composer and violinist Lodovico Sirmen. They toured Europe together and lived in London and Dresden and Paris. It is thought that the compositions that appeared under the name of both her and her husband are hers, as they are in a very different style from what he composed himself. Her string quartets are probably the first ever published by a woman. I remember reading that Mozart's father used to play them. But I've never seen them myself."

Roberta had been turning the pages of Anna Maria's book of scores. "What we need," she said thoughtfully, "is a bound book like this for a bassoonist. Even if it was only scores from Vivaldi, we might find her name and learn to recognize her style."

"That's much easier said than done," exclaimed Giovanna, gesturing to the stacks of shelves and boxes. "There could be something in this room like that. There are other rooms like this in the conservatory. And other museums. And more libraries, also filled with shelves and books." I could see, in Giovanna's eyes an Escher-like image of library corridors turning into shelves turning into boxes full of corridors.

"There must be another way," said Roberta.

"Patience is the only way," said Giovanna. "Patience, obsession, money perhaps. And only occasionally a little bit of luck. Or sheer coincidence."

Nicky repeated in a slightly discouraged voice, "or sheer coincidence." I felt the same on seeing all the boxes. Nicola, whatever her virtues, was not a particularly patient woman. I couldn't seriously imagine her taking time from her busy career to sit in a cramped Venetian library combing through piles of musical scores. After all, it had taken over two centuries to rediscover Vivaldi himself. And decades to catalog and reissue and record his immense productivity.

Giovanna was looking at her watch. "I am sorry," she said, hustling us politely from the room. "I wish we had more time. Another day perhaps," she said to Nicky. "Your girlfriend told us you are in a little bit of trouble."

"Cassandra is not my girlfriend," said Nicky, rather severely. "Is there a toilet up here? I'll join you downstairs in a moment."

"Of course."

Roberta, Giovanna and I traipsed down the marble staircase. From behind one of the doors came the tootling sounds of wood-winds warming up; from behind another a woman was singing an aria from *Aida*. "I feel as if I've seen bound volumes like that of Anna Maria's before," Roberta said as we went through the door to the campo outside.

"They could be in the Biblioteca Marciana," suggested Giovanna. "They could be there. They could be anywhere."

"Why, Cassandra," said Andrew McManus. "What are you doing here?" But he was staring at Roberta, obviously struck once again by her great similarity to her brother.

He was standing in the campo, in conversation with a stylish woman who was hanging chummily on his arm. He wore a corduroy jacket and carried a battered briefcase.

"Sightseeing," I said nervously. Nicky must be right behind us. I didn't want Andrew to see her.

"Oh. Well, I was just having lunch with the chief librarian here," said Andrew. "She's very interested in my research and is going to make the archives completely available to me. I'll have a student assistant and access to all the material. I'm so thrilled. And, she says she knows of a flat in her brother's building that is available."

"Giovanna," said the chief librarian. "I wonder if you can take Signore McManus up to the archives and give him a brief overview. He's looking for material on the girls of the Pietà, particularly the bassoonists."

"Bassoonists?" Giovanna said, looking surprised. "But . . ."

"There's a lot of interest now in the subject," I said to Giovanna, hoping she would interpret my look to understand that there was a rivalry between Nicky and Andrew and she must on no account help Andrew.

"I see," said Giovanna, and she gave me a wink as she led Andrew through the door. I had a feeling they would not be starting with the same boxes we had.

"Well," said Roberta. "I suppose I have to go back to work and sell *The Four Seasons* now." She paused. "I don't know if you would be interested, but I'm performing with another group tonight. We do klezmer music sometimes by the Ghetto. Perhaps you and Nicky would like to come."

"I'll ask her when she comes down." I was distracted by Nicky's

113

absence. Was she hiding to avoid Andrew?

"It's true what Nicky said?" Roberta pressed me. "You're not her girlfriend?"

"It's true," I said. "She owns a house in London, and she lets me have a room in the attic. We've had that arrangement for years."

"But you have had women lovers?" she asked.

"Oh yes." Roberta looked expectant. "Well, there was Angela most recently. I met her in Sydney. She was a brainy scientist type, but a fun-loving one. Or so I thought. Come along to the South Seas, she said, and who could resist?" I thought it best not to go into the details of our expedition. "That's how it is with me. They come, and they go. Some of them remain friends." How to explain that neither Nicky nor I really did the girlfriend bit? At least not for very long.

She was clearly fascinated, but a little disapproving. "My relationship with Francesca—it's the first time for her. We have only a few friends we can be at ease around. Giovanna is one. She's that way herself, though she doesn't have anybody."

"Francesca is a lovely girl," I said noncommittally.

"Yes, but you know our families don't like it. It's hard for us. Sometimes we think of going somewhere else to live in Italy or the world, like Canada. It's hard for us to imagine sharing an apartment here. Yet it's terrible that we can't be together."

"You and your father have quarreled for a long time. Getting a flat couldn't make it worse."

"That's true. And my brother thinks just the way my father does."

"Andrew believes your brother is gay."

"No! Well—it's possible. He doesn't have a girlfriend. He hasn't had one in a long while, it's strange. Maybe . . . but then why would he be so hard on me?"

"Frightened of losing your father perhaps."

I was hoping we might lead into more of a discussion about Marco and their father, but Roberta suddenly looked at her watch again and said, "Now I must go!"

There was still no sign of Nicky. She may have decided to talk with Andrew, perhaps to consider him not so much a competitor as an ally. I might as well leave. I found myself walking toward Francesca's shop. I wouldn't bother her. I would just buy some ink. I'd just look at her. But halfway there, I turned back. No, my path was renunciation. I still had a hundred pages of *Lovers and Virgins* to get through, and I still hadn't made up my mind whether it should be translated or not. I'd pick up a slice of pizza somewhere, go back to my hotel and spend the afternoon reading. Surely I'd done enough for one day. Perhaps later, if I felt like it, I'd try to look up Albert—to reassure myself he wasn't really the type to break into Nicky's house, if not to get to the bottom of his connection with the bassoon.

Back at the hotel I found two messages. One was from Anna: *Was the book useful? By the way, the inspector may be paying you a visit after lunch.*

The other was from Nicky. The clerk said she'd left it five minutes before: *Meet me at three at the Guggenheim Museum.*

I was tired of these peremptory messages from Nicky; and, besides, it was already two thirty and I'd been rushing around all day. Why couldn't she have just waited for me at the conservatory? How did she get here before me? I wanted to rest. I wanted to read my book. I wanted to mull over last night's events and decide whether I should accept an encore, should one be offered.

On the other hand, I did not particularly wish to speak to the Italian police.

Without going upstairs, I left the hotel and walked the few short blocks to the Peggy Guggenheim Collection.

Thirteen

I ARRIVED AT THE MUSEUM before Nicky and, after a quick cruise through the galleries hung with Klees and Kandinskys, returned to the sculpture garden. For just a moment I allowed myself to rest and breathe deeply. In the midst of Venice's concentrated stone warrens, the garden was a splash of restful greenery. Trees, bushes, graves. Graves? I'd seated myself on a small bench in front of a plaque that read "Here Rests Peggy Guggenheim." Next to it was another plaque, with a long, rather stupefying list of names under the mournful sentence: "Here Lie My Beloved Babies."

Their average age at death was only about ten, though some had been as young as three or four when they died. But this was horribly sad! Or perhaps just horrible. Had one of the Guggenheims really been a serial killer? It just went to show how the rich considered themselves above the law.

"They were her Lhasas, Cassandra," said Nicky, coming up to the bench. "Do you really think someone would name her children Cappuccino and Madame Butterfly?"

116

Nicky was still wearing her gray suit and brogues, but she'd added the most extraordinary pair of sunglasses, like something out of a Wonder Woman comic strip. She said she'd just bought them at the museum shop. They were a copy of Peggy's, and they made a strong impression with the curls Nicky had unleashed from the severe knot of an hour or so earlier.

We repaired to the sleek, white café and selected tortas and espresso. The café was hung with black and white photographs of Peggy and friends. None of the pictures had captions. Jean Cocteau, I guessed. Man Ray. And there was Peggy herself, in the sunglasses.

"I waited for you for ages outside the conservatory," I said. "What happened to you?"

"I had to escape a back way, Cassandra. It was a miracle Andrew didn't see me in the closed section."

"You weren't supposed to be in the closed section. You were supposed to be in the loo."

"I got lost, all right?" She patted her briefcase.

"What have you got in there, Nicky?"

"Just something I'd like to look at a little more closely."

"You can't just come to Italy and start appropriating things you take a fancy to, willy-nilly. Didn't you learn your lesson with that goddamn bassoon? Do you want to end up in an Italian prison? You're already on the run from the police. *And* you don't have a passport. Because you're certainly not using mine forever! I can't keep helping you, and that's final."

"Don't get your Jockeys in a twist, lass. Though if you'd really wanted to have been a help, you could have prevented me from buying this suit. It's lovely and all that, but the next time I'll wear it will be probably be at a funeral. It was absolutely the wrong thing to meet Giovanna in."

I was so speechless I could barely open my mouth when my pear torta was placed ceremoniously in front of me.

Nicky tucked into something very chocolate. "Really, Cassandra, I don't blame you, but I did have the impression I'd be dealing with a repressed old librarian and that it was essential to make a good impression and play the respectable Scotswoman. Then I see Giovanna is wearing a little pink dress like an ice cream cone . . ."

"That's enough from you, Nicola Gibbons. I've gone far beyond the call of duty. Hanging about in dusty old libraries, making a pest of myself with snotty young desk clerks, allowing myself to be . . . flirted with by all and sundry."

"All and sundry?" Nicky asked, savoring a large forkful of bitter-chocolate.

"Never mind," I said. "I don't want to talk about Giovanna or your other intrigues. I don't even want to know what you've got in that briefcase. Let's talk about your serious problem. I found that conductor's biography in your old room at the *palazzo* and looked through it. Don't you think there's a possibility that Olivia's son, Jakob, was not her husband's child? The conductor seems to hint that he and Olivia had known each other—known each other well, that is—for a very long time."

"I remembered something like that too. That's why I asked you to bring the book. But then I realized it wouldn't make any difference. No one disputes that Jakob was Olivia's son, that he married a girl named Elizabeth and that Bitten had a mother called Elizabeth. I hate to admit it, but I really think she might be Olivia's granddaughter. And I can't bear it. I absolutely can't bear it!"

Nicky put down her fork. It showed how awful she felt that she stopped eating.

"I know," I said, "the money, the house, everything that Olivia left you. But surely, the courts . . ."

"It's not the money, lass," said Nicky fiercely. "It's not even the house—as a house. It's too bloody huge, anyway, for one woman and that ne'er-do-well translator who occasionally deigns to inhabit her attic. It's the idea of losing the spirit of Olivia. Her music, my music—it's bound into the molecules of the walls. I couldn't bear to have that taken away. I don't know if I could even keep playing music if I couldn't play it there."

Tears rolled from under the Guggenheim glasses, down Nicky's full cheeks.

I said hesitantly, "You know, if you didn't treat Bitten as an enemy, you really might be able to work something out. It's a common human desire to know who you are and who your people are, where you come from. Why would Bitten want a house in London, anyway? She lives in Stockholm and seems well off. Maybe she'd like a few mementos. Even some sort of cash payment wouldn't be too bad, would it, not if you could stay in the house. She's not a monster, Nicky. And now she's lost Gunther. Their affair might have been brief, but obviously she's devastated."

"I can't cope with death," she said. "Not with Gunther's. It reminds me of Olivia's, and that's bad enough."

I knew she'd been the one to find Olivia's body. The old woman had fallen during a heart attack on her way to the bathroom late one night. Nicky had wakened immediately at the sound, but it was still too late.

"If you didn't fight that feeling, Nicky, you could relate to Bitten. If you made some small gesture of sympathy . . . Just from a practical point of view, Bitten could help you with the whole manuscript research problem . . ."

Nicky thought it over. "No," she said. "Gestures of sympathy are not my line. Every time I try to be sympathetic—to my mother or sisters, for instance—it backfires, and I end up in a worse position."

Since I'd had so much the same experience with my family, it was hard to argue.

"Olivia was my only real family—besides you," said Nicky. "She took me in, she loved me, she helped me. If I couldn't hold on to the sense of who we were to each other, I don't know what I'd do."

"I understand," I said. "You're my . . . real family too."

"Then why won't you move downstairs?"

"Because I never had my own room when I was growing up. I had all those tedious sisters. I don't want another sister!"

"You just said I was family to you."

"Can't you be my brother? Can't we just continue the way we are?"

"Oh, let's just drop it. Let's eat some more cake!" She called over the waiter, ordered another round, and opened the briefcase. "Now, no judging, Cassandra. I don't plan to keep this, just to look at it."

It was the bound volume of music by Anna Maria, the *maestra*.

"Giovanna may get in terrible trouble if you hold on to that. She doesn't know you took it, does she?"

"No, it was kind of a spur of the moment thing. I went to the loo and suddenly decided just to take another look in the special section. Then that bloody snoop Andrew appeared, and I panicked and grabbed it."

"Luckily you'll have a chance to see her tonight and return it," I said. "Roberta is playing music tonight and invited us. She said perhaps we could meet up with Giovanna beforehand at my hotel and all go over together."

Nicky was now deep into her second slice of chocolate torta. "Of course, I'd love to go. But it's so tiresome, the thought that I have to go shopping again this afternoon. I can't wear this suit, and everything else is at the Sandrettis'. Plus I need to keep *somewhat* in disguise. Maybe . . . a cloak? But I really don't want to look like a big thundercloud. If only you would let me wear your beret. I think I could organize a look around that beret."

I was about to tell her I couldn't care less what she wore, but that she certainly was not making off with my beret, when I spotted two people I knew—whom we both knew—in the sculpture garden. They were coming toward the café.

"Keep down," I said, no easy task for a woman close to two hundred pounds with hair even wilder than mine. I snatched the Peggy Guggenheim glasses off her nose. "I'll keep them busy while you sneak out the exit by the gift shop. Throw down some money."

"All right," said Nicky, and yanked at my beret.

"Hey," I yelled, but it was too late. I rushed toward Anna de Hoog and Marco before they could come up the terrace steps. "Darlings," I said, "how absolutely divine to see you again."

"Cassandra?" asked Marco. "You look . . . different."

"Yes, it's my new look. What do you think?"

"I like the glasses," said Marco. "Your hair . . . I have only seen you wearing your beret." He paused diplomatically. "It is . . . big."

"Cassandra's hair is wonderful," said Anna. She had been looking over my shoulder in the direction I'd just come from, but now she gave me her full attention. I must admit, her full attention made me shiver. That and the fact she was finally out of that frumpy skirt and into some Levi's and a crisp shirt with a sweater tied at her shoulders. "It's very Leonore Fini."

Marco was looking uneasy, but he was too polite to indicate that my being in Nicky's room this morning might have anything to do with the way Anna was looking at me.

"What brings the two of you here?" I asked.

"Frigga is lying down," said Anna. "So I thought I'd ask Marco to be my guide here for an hour or two. Just for a break. Being at the *palazzo* when Frigga is wandering around and weeping is a little like being in a Greek tragedy."

"It is stressful," Marco allowed. "She feels it very deeply, his death."

"No further leads on what exactly happened to Gunther?"

"No," said Anna. "No signs of struggle. He wasn't drunk. He had some bruises on his head, but he probably got those when he fell. They're still treating it as an accident. So none of us are suspects exactly, and yet we all are."

Marco sighed. "I think, perhaps he was involved in drugs or something. That phone always ringing."

"They would like to question you, Cassandra," said Anna. "I don't know if you saw the note I left for you at the hotel."

"They will await you at the *palazzo* at four," said Marco.

I wondered if Anna had seen the note from Nicky to me. I wondered if that was why she was here. I wondered what was the real reason she'd brought Marco with her.

"I guess I'll go back to the *palazzo* then," I said, resolving to do no such thing. "Of course, I have nothing to hide."

"Of course not," said Anna.

The Lista di Spagna, with its jumble of hotels, overpriced trattorias and souvenir kiosks, was hardly the area I'd expect Albert to be staying. But when I asked at a bar near the train station for a hotel that used to be a monastery, I was directed down a narrow street, and almost immediately the noise of the Lista di Spagna faded. No one was at the desk when I entered, so I wandered through a marble-floored grand hall to a garden. Fig trees and pines scented the air along with roses and orange trees. I heard birds for the first time since my arrival in Venice.

The place suited Albert better than the Danieli, I thought, and then wondered how I could know. I hardly knew Albert at all. Our time in the Norwegian fjord country had been more competitive than social, and I'd spent only one evening with him since. I was pretty sure he was not a murderer, but I was sure of nothing else.

Back at the desk I was told, regretfully, that Signore Egmont was out, and no, they had no idea where he was or when he might be back. But if Madame would like to leave a message?

Madame wrote on a piece of hotel stationery, "What the hell are you up to, Albert?"

But I was still left with the problem of what to do now. I did not particularly want to go back to my hotel and be questioned by the police. I would feel obligated to give them the name of Nicky's pension, and she might find herself in real trouble. Why hadn't she just stayed in England when she had the chance? Aside from wanting to know about the bassoon and Gunther, the inspector would be asking questions about how she came to re-enter the country with a stolen passport. My passport.

Where to, then? I began walking up the Fondamenta di Cannaregio, which, before the train station was built, was the main entrance to Venice. The Cannaregio had fallen off somewhat since then. The nicest thing about it was that, since it didn't have many famous sites, there were far fewer tourists. It was dirtier here, more pungent. The air smelled of fish frying in olive oil, of garlic and tomatoes, of faintly brackish water. I walked until I saw the sign for the Ghetto, and turned off the *fondamenta*. I followed the street past woodworking shops and a kosher restaurant or two to the Campiello delle Scole. Then I came to the footbridge that led to the Ghetto Nuovo. In spite of its name, the Ghetto Nuovo was not new at all. It was the original Jewish ghetto in Venice, the compulsory residence from which all subsequent ghettos derived their name, *geto*, the Venetian word for foundry.

This bridge was one of three that connected the island to the rest of Venice. Connected and closed off. For three centuries the gated bridges had been locked at night, for protection, some said. At one time several thousand Jews had lived on the enclosed island, Ashkenazim and later Sephardim. When Napoleon ordered the gates torn down, that number dropped, though the Jews of the city still continued to pray and do business in the Ghetto.

The large campo seemed a peaceful place this late afternoon, with a few well-dressed children tossing a ball back and forth, their grandparents chatting on a bench. Compared to most places in Venice, it was so quiet that it was hard to imagine a time when the square would have been packed with bankers, laundresses, jewelers, rag and bone pickers, rabbinical students. With children playing games.

The golden light of Venice fell on the Holocaust memorial along one wall.

I walked over to a corner of the square to the museum, paid for a ticket and went upstairs. I was weary suddenly, more melancholy than was proper for a truly inspired museum visit. Yet I didn't know what else to do at the moment.

A man was standing with his back to me in front of a glass display case. I didn't recognize him immediately because a yarmulke covered his bald head and his hands were in the pockets of his cloth coat. But after I watched him a moment, I realized there could be no mistake. His reflection floated eerily among the filigreed silver prayer books, the elaborate pitchers, the worked-silver scroll cases and the branched candelabras.

He felt himself observed, turned easily and smiled with more pleasure than worry. It was almost as if he'd planned that I'd follow him to this obscure campo and tiny museum filled with silver liturgical objects.

"Cassandra, my dear. Are you here for the tour as well?"

Fourteen

"No, I'M NOT HERE for the tour!" I said. "I'm here to ask you some questions."

"No need to blurt. We have plenty of time, my dear," he said, putting a black-gloved hand on one of my waving arms. "We can talk while we're being shown about. I've been looking forward to this tour of the Ghetto's synagogues for ages. I like what you've done with your hair, by the way. It seems to have grown since I saw you last."

"Humidity," I muttered.

"Yes, I expect a storm is coming," Albert said. "The air feels quite tingly."

He had led me firmly down the stairs to the group standing in the forecourt of the museum. Almost everyone looked American to me, and few of the couples seemed to be traveling well.

"We could of bought the same exact menorah at home, Daniel," one frosted blonde was chiding her husband.

There were five synagogues for us to visit. When the Jews were moved on to the small island they'd had to take what buildings were given them, but over the years they had modified the interiors and extended the number of stories on the houses. The *scola*, or synagogues, meeting houses for public prayers as well as general assembly halls and study halls for the daily reading of the Torah, were usually on the top floor of a house, with five windows visible from the outside. Only those five windows gave an indication from the campo that a holy place was hidden above.

We trudged up some back stairs to the Scola Canton, a jewel-box of a synagogue built in the early 1500s. Inside, it was like being in an ornate Renaissance chest, all inlaid with wood and decorated with small paintings illustrating stories from the Bible. Albert had taken out tiny binoculars and put them to his eyes to more closely inspect Moses parting the Red Sea. Questions peppered the guide, a young woman with a streak of orange through her otherwise sedately styled dark hair. Did the Ashkenazim speak Yiddish here? Yes, they did. They were poorer than the Levantines, who came later and were Mediterranean merchants, and the Sephardim, who were ousted from Spain, but who brought wealth with them as well as a habit of praying in secret. The Ashkenazim had been forced since medieval times to be the bank for the poor as well as the rich. I listened with half an ear while I considered what I really wanted to know from Albert.

As the yarmulkes swarmed, I mentally reviewed what I knew of the recent events.

A rare bassoon belonging to Signore Sandretti had been stolen from Nicola's room while she was sleeping. Although the bassoon was mysteriously recovered by Albert, Sandretti had claimed he didn't recognize it. The evening of the bassoon's attempted return, Gunther was found dead in the canal. Anna de Hoog was first on the scene, followed by Sandretti. I knew Gunther had left the Pietà during Act Two of *Orlando Furioso* after receiving a phone call, and Bitten had followed him. She said they took a walk, in the direction of the naval museum. They were observed in the act of quarreling by Marco and Andrew, who'd left the performance during the interval between Acts Two and Three. Marco and Andrew then walked in the opposite direction and went to the bar of the Danieli for a drink. That left about a half an hour for someone to push Gunther into the canal.

Bitten had the opportunity, but unless she was someone other than who she said she was, unless she had been faking an attraction to Gunther, unless he had so roused her to anger that she considered killing him, she didn't really have the motivation. That's what it came down to.

"Let's get one thing out of the way," Albert said, sidling up. "Then you can stop giving me those terribly suspicious looks. Tell me you don't suspect me of murdering Gunther."

"No," I said grudgingly. "You were with me the whole time."

"And it's precisely for that reason that I don't suspect you."

"Me!"

We left the Scola Canton and started downstairs with the rest of the group. In front of us were Daniel and his wife, still arguing about the menorah. About whether the one they had bought, that Daniel Big-Spender had bought, was the exact replica of one easily found at Bloomingdales. For half the price.

"Here's my question to you," said Albert. "Who called Gunther on his cell phone during the concert?"

"Frigga, I assume."

"And she is?"

"His great-grandmother. She raised him after his mother died. She arrived in Venice yesterday."

"It would be easy enough," said Albert, "to check the cell phone and see what the last number on it was."

"Except that the cell phone went into the drink with him."

The tour guide was now leading us up another set of stairs in another building. Some impatient male members of the group had taken off their yarmulkes, and the guide reminded them they had to put them on again. This synagogue was crimson and dark wood. It too was small and had a hidden feeling.

"Where was the elder Sandretti during the concert?" asked Albert, and then darted away to observe some carvings close up.

I waited until the guide had finished her description, and then closed in on Albert again. Signore Sandretti had definitely been there at the beginning—he'd introduced the opera—and at the end, but I hadn't seen him, at all, during the concert.

"But why would Sandretti murder Gunther?" I whispered to Albert, as the group began to leave the room.

Albert was still enthralled by the wooden bas-reliefs. With difficulty he put his binoculars down and turned to me, sighing. "I'm not suggesting that. I'm only saying that he is not what he seems."

"Because of the bassoon?"

"Exactly. Here we have a well-known Venetian musical impresario, whom one suspects might be in a little financial difficulty. He reports that a bassoon has disappeared. Not just any rare bassoon from a museum, but a bassoon from his private collection. A bassoon that he repeatedly asserts is a musical instrument once used by the Pietà performers and one which has been in the family for generations."

"Don't you believe him?"

"That's hardly for me to say. But I suspect that his assertion adds to the value of the instrument. That's usually why people make such assertions. Perhaps he even has some documentation to back up his claim. No, the interesting question has always been, why was this particular bassoon taken?"

"To get Nicky in trouble," I said promptly. We were walking en masse down the street that led off the island and connected the old enclosed Ghetto with the area where the Sephardim had moved. Once it had been open and farmlike, according to the guide, with an inn and various shops. Now it was as dense as any place in Venice. We passed the shop where Daniel had apparently purchased the menorah. "No, I am not exchanging it. This is not New York; it is not a department store kind of mentality, Doris!"

I added, "Bitten stole it to punish Nicky for . . . something. A jealousy thing."

"Ah, the psychological factor," Albert said. "And yet there may be a far simpler explanation."

"Such as?"

"Insurance, my sweet. If a rare bassoon from a museum had been stolen, it would have been a serious offense as well as a loss to the Italian people—not exactly on the order of a Bellini Madonna being stolen in broad daylight from a church, but a loss all the same—but it would not have personally enriched Signore Sandretti."

"Which might explain why Sandretti claimed the bassoon wasn't his when you returned it." I thought back to that peculiar scene. "Bitten and Marco recognized it immediately."

"Marco strikes me as unhealthily loyal to his father," Albert said. "I'm not sure what Bitten's silence meant."

"The psychological factor again?" I suggested. "She wanted Nicky to be guilty."

"Psychology is all very well," said Albert as we stepped into the last synagogue on the tour, a small one below that of the Levantines, which was closed to visitors. "But in my profession, money is usually the great motivator."

"Even for murder?"

"I have seen it happen," said Albert, enigmatically.

When the tour was over, we stepped out into the silvery stone street of late afternoon. The clouds above were pink and thunder blue: cool colors, in spite of the retained warmth of the pavement and houses. The air rumbled quietly, as if to itself, as if contemplating further action.

The guide's talk in the last small family synagogue had sobered us. For she had told us about the rounding up of Venice's Jews during the war. Compared to Germany and Poland, the numbers were minuscule; still, only sixty people returned. The population had remained small in the Ghetto. There were no Ashkenazim left, only Sephardim. Daniel and Doris were no longer arguing, I noticed, and several people wiped away tears.

As Albert and I walked back in the direction of the campo, I asked, "But how did you come up with the bassoon in the first place? And where is it now?"

"Since we're in the neighborhood," he said, "I suggest we pay a visit to my old friend Graciela."

Graciela's antique shop was a tiny, tasteful place in a quiet square nearby. It was not overly stuffed with objects like many stores of its nature, where you find potato mashers rolled up in Turkish rugs, African masks thrown into Mexican baskets along with broken toys and silver-plated pepper mills. Here one would not discover any odd treasures like a box of doll's heads or an old travel book titled *By Camel Across the Desert, by Two Ladies.* In Graciela's shop, the display was deliberate, not random. A few silver teaspoons tied together, a mottled green flask of hand-blown glass, a single delicate wine glass of a beautiful rose color, a spill of glass beads. On a velvet scarf was arranged a handful of old jewelry that made me think of the once frivolous dead. On the walls were nails with coat hangers from which swung a few garments: two embroidered men's coats, one faded red, one sky blue, a sateen vest that suggested Regency England, some silk scarves from the Orient.

Graciela came forward and kissed Albert three times on the cheeks. "My dear," she said in perfect English. "I did not expect to see you again today."

"Graciela, *cara*," said Albert. "My dear friend Cassandra, whom I ran into *quite* unexpectedly and who has been the source of all this whirlwind woodwind business, has some questions that I thought we could answer together."

"Certainly," said Graciela, motioning us onto three rickety but beautiful eighteenth-century chairs. Graciela was not like some of the secondhand dealers I'd known and loved over the years, the shabby and eccentric purveyors of all that was useless, abandoned and mysteriously compelling. Not only was she coiffed and elegantly dressed, but Graciela had the precise gestures and regal manners of a duchess. She reminded me, oddly, of Olivia Wulf, except that her smile was genuine and her voice more kind than gruff. She was a bit older than Albert, I guessed, but then, I had no real idea how old Albert was. He could be thirty-five; he could be sixty.

"Cassandra would like to know how the bassoon came to you," Albert prompted, since I seemed suddenly tongue-tied.

"Of course. When Albert told me what he was looking for, I put the word out immediately, especially among my colleagues who specialize in old musical instruments. I didn't have much hope, to tell the truth. Generally whatever is stolen in Italy is out of the country within twenty-four hours. To my surprise I got a call back very quickly. My friend Andreas said that a gondolier had brought the bassoon in two days ago, saying it had been left under a seat. It appeared to have been privately owned. It had no museum markings at any rate. I called Albert, and he retrieved it from my colleague and brought it to the Sandretti *palazzo*. It wasn't a question of selling it back to Sandretti, of course; still, we did expect a small gift, a token, for our help and honesty."

Albert nodded, his domed head gilded in the chandelier light. "When Sandretti refused to accept the bassoon or even acknowledge that he recognized it, I realized something else was going on."

"A gondola!" I said. "Isn't there a Lost and Found for gondola boats?"

They both laughed politely.

"What did you do with the bassoon before the concert then?"

"As you suspected, I placed it in the Danieli's left luggage room with my friend the porter, who was under strict instructions to report to me if anyone came asking about it and also to deny that it was there. The next morning I picked it up and brought it here to Graciela's for safekeeping." Albert paused. "Three people came to the left luggage room to ask about it."

"I bet I can guess. Marco, Bitten and Sandretti."

"Partially right. Bitten came first. About a half hour later, Marco inquired. But the third person was not Sandretti. It was Anna de Hoog, who came after the concert. It was while she was asking about the bassoon that the doorman on the Danieli dock discovered Gunther's body in the canal."

"Which is why Anna was first at the scene of the crime," I said. "Sandretti and Anna de Hoog must be in this together somehow. Is that why you left me the note at the hotel asking what orchestras she played with?"

"A word in your ear, no more," said Albert. "As several people have noticed, Anna de Hoog is not the world's most remarkable musician."

I blushed, recalling the previous night. She had completely disarmed (and disrobed) me.

Graciela brought out the bassoon from the back of the room. "It would be curious indeed if this were one of the instruments from the Pietà. My colleague who specializes in musical instruments says that the Correr Museum owns and displays many of the instruments from the musical school of that *ospedale*. There are a number of violins as well as horns and flutes and oboes. There is even a pianoforte. But there are no bassoons among the inventory." She patted it somewhat regretfully. "I would not think of selling this, of course. I really hate to see beautiful and historical examples of the national patrimony leave the country."

"What about all this?" I gestured to the shelves around me. Did she think I was simple? The woman had an antique shop.

"Oh, very little of this is Italian," smiled Graciela. "Most of it comes from my visits to the big auctions in Great Britain, in the north of England and Scotland, particularly. That is how Albert and I met, didn't we?"

"But, but," I said, "Don't people come into your shop, your shop in *Venice*, expecting to buy something *Venetian?*"

"Collectors don't think that way, my sweet," Albert said with amusement. "And as for ordinary people . . ."

"They don't think about value and appreciation," said Graciela. "They love what they love. They love what speaks to them."

I looked around. The only thing that spoke to me in the shop was Graciela herself, but that was out of the question. Actually, the bassoon spoke to me as well. It said, "Give me to Nicky. *She'll* appreciate me."

I said, "I'll need to get Nicola over here. She could definitely recognize the bassoon. I mean, officially. At least that would get her out of being accused of theft." I looked around again. "She might recognize some other things. She's from Scotland, from a family that sold off quite a bit, I believe, on their descent from castle-living a few generations back."

"Some fall and some rise," said Albert, with a wink. I gathered he considered that he and I were among the latter. As he showed no signs of wishing to leave, I got up without having destroyed the antique chair and made my way to the door. This hardly seemed the place, in front of his elegant lady friend, to ask him the question I'd saved for last: *You wouldn't by any chance have noticed that the combination to Nicky's safe is kept in the lentil jar?*

"If you're not going to sell the bassoon and you're not going to give it back to the Sandrettis, at least right away, what are you going to do with it?"

"I'll keep it safe here," said Graciela.

"I had an uncle who was a tuba-player," said Albert. "Perhaps now is my chance to carry on the family talent for tooting. I might take up the bassoon. Just might. After all, it's one of my favorite instruments."

"Why?"

"Of all the instruments in the orchestra, it is the most emotionally distinctive. Other instruments, the piano and the violin for instance, have far greater tonal range. Yet what other instrument can alternate between bittersweet lyricism and outright jocularity with such engaging finesse?"

"Are you quoting someone, Albert?"

"Magazine article by Andrew McManus."

"And where would you have come across an article by Andrew McManus?"

"Stuffed inside the bassoon, oddly enough." Albert held a crumpled piece of newsprint. "Can't think how it got inside the tube."

Fifteen

I DIDN'T FIND ANNA de Hoog or, for that matter, Andrew or Bitten at the *palazzo* when I went by.

"Miss de Hoog took them out on an excursion to the cemetery," said the unhappy Marco. He was back to baby-sitting Frigga, who had slept for a while, but was now up and pacing again. We could hear her overhead. "San Michele is a very interesting island in the lagoon."

That Anna had some sly reason for taking Andrew and Bitten to the cemetery island of San Michele, I had no doubt. Still, I didn't think she would actually do away with them. Nor were they the characters in this drama I was most worried about.

"The police inspector came by here looking for you at four o'clock," Marco added. "He waited for a while, but then he left. He gives you his card and respectfully asks that you call him as soon as you can."

"Thanks. Listen, why don't you slip out for a drink, Marco? I'll go up and sit with Frigga a while."

"I am only gone a half hour, no more," said Marco gratefully. "I am only around the corner."

"Take your time." Not only did I wish to speak to Frigga, but I was curious about the library at the top of the stairs. I had caught only a glimpse when Sandretti opened it the other day, but I wondered if there might not be some interesting things in the desk or on the shelves, and not just the collected works of Plutarch.

But the door to the library was firmly locked, and no amount of jiggling would open it. Instead, I knocked on Frigga's door and, after a moment, went in.

The overhead light wasn't on, only a small lamp by the bed. Frigga stood, still in her Chanel suit, by the window watching the sunset over the Giudecca Canal. The gathering storm had brought piles of blue-black clouds, embroidered with gold thread.

"I was in Venice as a girl," she said, half turning to see who it was, and then turning back. She spoke in German, and I had to strain to understand. "I came with my father and mother in the twenties. They were prosperous then, at least enough to take an Italian holiday. We stayed on the Lido, not here in the city. The city was thought to be unhealthy. We stayed at the Excelsior. I remember my father saying we would return here often. But of course we never did. The economy turned very bad, and my father lost his factory. I married. Hitler came to power. I sent my daughter to Vienna to study, to be safe. She was safe. For a little while."

I'd charged in meaning to interrogate Frigga. After the tour of the synagogues, I hadn't been feeling particularly friendly toward members of the German population. Now I took a seat on the bed. The room was quite dark; only Frigga, small and almost young-looking stood out, silhouetted against a window full of black clouds and streaks of color, was in focus. Speaking in her own language, not in haltingly correct English, she was clear and fully herself.

136

"What happened to your daughter?" I asked, when she said no more. My German was not brilliant, but it was good enough to understand her story. What I did not understand, the sadness of history filled in for me.

"Dorothea was a music student at the conservatory in Vienna. She married, quite suddenly, a Jew who was a fellow student. He should have left when he had the chance. But something happened, he did not. Shortly after, he was arrested. He died in Dachau a year later, though I did not find that out for a long time. He simply disappeared. Dorothea came home to me in Munich, pregnant. During the war she died in a fire. I took the child and moved to a small village near the Rhine, with relatives.

"Ruth was all I had. My husband was shot very early on in the war. There was no chance of remarrying. We were scraping to live, for years and years. Ruth was my life, and yet I could not stop her from suffering. She suffered to be an orphan, she suffered because she was a girl of much talent, she suffered because she was half Jewish. She grew up hating everyone. Her life was a tragedy. She could have been a musician like her parents. She had the skill and the temperament. If she had not lived in this village. If we had had money, or someone to help us after the war. Instead, she threw herself away, at only twenty. She threw herself away with a boy in the village who cared nothing for her. She was a sensitive, beautiful girl, like her mother. She had a baby, and the shame was too much for her. She killed herself."

Frigga had wrapped her arms around herself tightly, and rocked back and forth. There was very little light now. In the distance there was lightning. The air was close in the room.

"I resolved I would bring up her little boy and do everything I could do for him that I had not done for Ruth. The times were better then. He went to an excellent school, he received a scholarship to

137

study music at the university. He was a good and faithful son to me, who always called and who never went with bad girls. That is why I do not believe he was engaged to this Swedish woman. Not after knowing her only a week. He told me nothing about it."

"Did he call you from Venice?"

"Oh yes, several times. He described it beautifully. He said I should come. I said, no, I was too old to travel. Too old to travel to Venice." She laughed with some bitterness. She came away from the window finally and turned on a lamp. Our eyes blinked in the sudden light.

"You didn't happen to call the evening he was . . . found?"

"I never called him," said Frigga. "I didn't have to. He called me."

"But I heard his phone ring several times. I heard him talking to someone he called Frigga."

She looked astonished and then hurt and then firm again. "But he would never have called me Frigga," she said. "He always called me *Grossmutter*, just as Ruth had."

Marco knocked and came in. He still looked worried. "You will join us for dinner I hope, Mrs. Reilly."

"Sorry," I said, looking at my watch, "I have plans for the evening. But I would very much like to speak with Anna de Hoog." I scribbled down the name of the restaurant where the klezmer band was to play. "Perhaps she could join me there when she returns from the cemetery."

I said good-bye to Frigga with more gentleness than I'd shown when barreling into her room earlier. Marco followed me down the stairs.

"You know, Mrs. Reilly, the police . . . "

"It's all right, Marco. I won't be telling the police what I know. I won't reveal your deep, dark secret."

I meant it for a joke, but he stared at me, shocked. "I have no secret."

I felt sorry for him—conflicted about his sexuality, obviously in thrall to his father and Sandretti's devious financial machinations, despised, perhaps rightly, by his strong-minded sister. "About Andrew," I said impulsively. "I hope the two of you . . ."

But that seemed only to alarm him more, though he tried to hide it.

Giovanna and I had arranged by phone that Nicky and I would meet her at her aunts' restaurant in a small campo near the Via Garibaldi, away from the main tourist areas near the public gardens. There we'd have dinner and then stroll over to the Ghetto to hear Roberta and her klezmer group.

Not surprisingly, Nicky was practicing when I arrived. It was something I recognized, one of those Vivaldi largos or andantes that separated the first and third allegro movements of just about every bassoon concert I'd ever heard of his. It did no good to ask Nicky which concerto it was, because she always said No. 18 or No. 12, which gave me no mnemonic clue. But for some of them, I had my own secret names; this one was "The Snake" since it had a lovely sinuous longing to it. I didn't knock until she finished that movement; then I barged in. The first thing I did was to take my Canadian Mounties' beret off the chair post and stuff my hair back inside it.

"Giovanna awaits," I said.

"Right," she said, tossing the bassoon aside and searching for her shoes, a newly purchased pair of silver boots with impossibly high heels.

"Nicky!" I said. "We're going to have to walk."

"I can walk. Besides, I adore these boots, and I need to erase the image of those hideous brogues from Giovanna's mind."

She ripped the beret off my head and started pulling at the sleeves of my bomber jacket.

"Hey, leave off," I protested.

"I want to see you in a cape I just bought."

She threw open the wardrobe and hauled out a long black velvet cape with a hood. It was beautiful, but it was her, not me.

"Cassandra, live a little. Forget the beret. Find your inner Venetian. Put on the cape, lass. See, you look *exactly* like me, especially with the hood over your head."

"Oh, is that the plan, then?" I said.

"Well you're the one who wants me to go out," she said, tugging on the bomber jacket. "To go where I could well be recognized." Panting, she tried to zip up the jacket.

"Don't break the zipper!" I warned. I was quite liking the feel of the velvet, though I would never have admitted it. I threw it off and wrestled the beret from her head and the jacket from her back.

The rain still held off as we set out, but the air was violent, and the sky crackled. I was not going much faster than Nicky. After all, I had been on my feet nearly all day, had hardly had a proper meal, and was still carrying the conductor's biography as well as the two novels in my satchel, and one of the novels was very heavy.

"Oh, just toss them," Nicky said when I complained. "Tell Simon both of them are dreadful. He'll never know."

"The whole issue," I said, ignoring that suggestion, "is what sort of literature should be published. I'm being asked to decide, and I can't. One of these is entertaining and one isn't. One of these is profound, and the other is superficial, but with some feminist interest. But literature can't just be entertaining."

"Why not?" asked Nicky. She was absolutely the wrong person

to discuss this with. She adored historical romance novels, particularly if they had dramatic Highland settings, and the men were called "the Bruce" and wore short skirts, and the women defended their castles with pots of boiling pitch. She'd probably love *Lovers and Virgins*.

"Entertainment is not enough," I said. "It's enough sometimes. You don't want to hear the Beatles fully orchestrated. You don't want Aretha singing *Tosca*. But serious literature is so much *better*. So much *deeper*. So much . . ."

"You take the high road and I'll take the low road," hummed Nicky.

"Well, you won't be there before me in those ridiculous shoes," I snapped.

"Oh, come along, Grandma," said Nicky, pushing me on to the *vaporetto* at San Tomà and into a seat. "The best art is entertaining *and* serious. Like Vivaldi. Like Matisse. Like a big, beautiful woman wearing high heels."

"With analogies like that, it's a good thing you're a bassoonist and not a poet," I said, but "Grandma" had made me think of "Grossmutter."

I told Nicky about my conversation with Frigga. As I talked I was conscious of a word or two lying just below the surface in my memory. Something someone had said, or that I'd read, that hadn't quite jibed.

"That's incredibly sad," she said. "I couldn't see Gunther for Bitten. It's strange, isn't it, how they both were marked by the war? Bitten lost her father in Dachau and Gunther his grandfather."

We had the brightly lit Palladian rectangle of the Church of the Redentore on our right and the sweep of San Marco's waterfront, the Molo, with its stairs leading down into the lagoon, its view into the Piazza, coming up in front of us. The front door of Venice, it had

141

been called. It still astonished me whenever I saw it. Nicky didn't look at the glorious view, however, but directly at me. I could see she was thinking over what I'd told her, and was worried.

Music students in Vienna. Attempts to get to London. Dachau.

"But Bitten's mother, Jakob's wife, was named Elizabeth," Nicky said. "Bitten and Gunther can't have been related, can they?"

"Gunther's grandmother was Frigga's daughter, Dorothea," I said. "She didn't go to Sweden, she went to Munich and died in a fire."

"And she didn't have a girl called Bitten. She had a daughter called Ruth, who was raised by Frigga."

"In wartime, there must be so many similar cases," I said uneasily.

"And anyway," said Nicky. "Someone would have contacted Olivia if Jakob had had children in Germany."

"Bitten's mother never tried to contact Olivia."

"There is no way Gunther and Bitten could be related—unless Jakob had two wives," Nicky said. As soon as she said it, dismissively, we both thought of Gunther's height and blondness, and how similar Bitten was. If Gunther's grandfather was named Jakob, that would make him Bitten's—what—half-nephew?

"If Bitten *is* Olivia's granddaughter," I said, as our boat began to travel along the length of the city to our stop at Giardini, "It's amazing that she's a bassoonist, just like you."

"No, not like me, Cassandra," said Nicky, almost harshly. "Because I *knew* Olivia, I cared for her, I loved her. Bitten never even met her."

142

Sixteen

I HAVE FRIENDS who moon over picture calendars of rural Tuscany, and save their money to rent villas outside Florence for a week or two in autumn and return home with bottles of wine and freshly pressed olive oil and longings to live *la dolce vita* permanently. These Italy-worshipping friends would never think of visiting Venice. It's too crowded, they say. It's too expensive. It's cold and haughty and damp and putrid-smelling. And, worst of all, it's the one place in Italy you can't even get a good meal.

But those people have clearly never eaten at a steamy little trattoria run by Giovanna's aunts, two energetic ladies in their sixties who kept the dishes coming for a good two hours: artichokes served with lemon and olive oil, followed by pumpkin gnocchi with a sauce of butter and sage. For Nicky, the heartless carnivore, there was a tender slice of veal Marsala, and for me, a lightly grilled local fish. Giovanna was presented with an array of vegetarian plates: roasted eggplant, crisp green beans, white beans with black olives. The aunts filled our glasses with Pinot Grigio, and at the end of the meal brought plates of fresh figs along with golden *vin santo*.

The aunts clearly approved of Nicky. They liked her auburn ring-lets and hearty appetite. They ran their hands over her silver lamé tunic and exclaimed when they heard she was a bassoonist. "Nicola, Nicolina," they were soon calling her, while their tongues twisted on Cassandra. "Eat, eat," they cooed, as Nicky cleaned her plate. They nudged Giovanna, "Another musician, hmmm?"

Giovanna took it in stride. Her little pink dress was gone, and, surprisingly, her strawberry hair had taken on a darker tint since this afternoon. She'd replaced her big green-rimmed glasses with wire-rims and was wearing a linen jacket over jeans. She had clearly tried to replicate Nicky's respectability even as Nicky had gone in the opposite direction to match Giovanna's earlier verve.

At the door there were embraces and kisses. The aunts handed Giovanna her violin case and our coats. They had Nicky in my leather jacket and me in her flowing velvet cloak before I could stop them.

"Relax, Cassandra," said Nicky when I began to protest. "Your inner Venetian, remember."

Outside in the small campo, the air was unstable, eager, and from an upper window came a woman's voice, singing. With the wind flapping the cloak around me, we began to walk down the Via Garibaldi to the embankment that ran along the lagoon. Giovanna and Nicola, deep in a discussion of Vivaldi, linked arms. The cama-raderie of musicians was something I'd always envied. Painters couldn't paint together, writers couldn't write; but whenever you got two musicians together, they always wanted to play something, sing something, even just hum.

We were strolling toward the Pietà. Over the last few days, I'd approached the church from the other direction, battling through tourists and vendors. From this direction everything was far less crowded; the heart of Venice, the Piazza, lay in front of us, but distant enough so that we saw only the lights, and didn't hear the babble of language. The sound of Venice tonight was the gurgle of the lagoon waters against the stone retaining walls, the faint buzz of motor boats, Giovanna's voice humming an example from some movement or other.

I caught up with the two of them in time to hear Nicky quoting, "'The canals are crowded with musical people at night, bands of music, French horns, duet singers in every gondola.' 1745, Dr. Charles Burney. He was an English musicologist who gave us a picture of Venetian musical life at that time, especially the women's orchestras of the *ospedali*. I'm thinking about using his words in the opening scenes of the film, as the camera pans over the city in an aerial shot, with gondolas arriving in front of the Pietà."

Only this morning the project had been a CD-ROM; in the library Nicky had begun talking of a video documentary. Now it was a film.

"You might show the audience going through the doors of the church of the Pietà," suggested Giovanna. "Lots of talking and bustle. Eighteenth-century dress, gold and velvet and silk in the candlelight. Slowly we become aware of the girls, all dressed in white, in the balconies above."

Nicky continued, "The camera focuses on the faces of the various girls as they tune up. The audience quiets. Vivaldi raises his baton. There's a long close-up of one girl, a bassoonist, raising the instrument to her lips. And then another voice-over, in her words: 'I never expected to find myself a performer in an all-women's orchestra . . .'"

"And now a flashback to a room where her mother, a celebrated courtesan, is giving birth . . ." Giovanna made some baby noises.

"The mother gives her baby an agonized look, and then turns away. 'Take her to the Pietà. At least let her have a different life than I can give her, than I had!'"

"A shot, a shot right here," Giovanna said excitedly, for by now we'd arrived at the Pietà itself, "of the baby going through the little door in the wall. The maid gives the sign of the cross as she places the baby inside and rings the bell. Then we see the baby being received on the other side by a nun. The baby is washed, marked with a small *P*. 'Your name will be . . .'"

"Giovanna," said Nicky.

"Isn't it time we should be getting to the klezmer concert?" I asked.

"No, it's early yet," said Giovanna. "Let's go inside a moment."

Very often the church had concerts at night; this was one of the few evenings it was empty. There was a soft rope stretched across the entrance to the church interior, but Giovanna persuaded the sacristan that Nicky was a famous filmmaker from London. At least I think that's what she said, for she spoke to the man in dialect.

It wasn't a particularly magnificent church, yet with imagination it was possible to people the space with chairs, not pews, and to place flickering wax candles on the walls instead of electric bulbs. It was possible to peer up and see the girls peering back through the grilles of the balconies above.

"And she looks out and sees her real mother," said Giovanna and added, sighing, "Isn't that what we all wish!"

"Yes," said Nicky, taking up the story. "Her mother is now old, raddled from syphilis, no longer able to work as a prostitute to the wealthy. She's dying, in fact, but she's come to see her daughter play the bassoon one last time."

"Now, Nicolina, are you absolutely firm that the focus of your film is the bassoon? Because Vivaldi was a great violinist, you know. Will there be perhaps some *small* role for a girl who is a violinist?"

I sat down in one of the pews, wrapping the long velvet cloak closely around me. They definitely had the right idea with these capes, those old Venetians. It had always seemed from the paintings that they wrapped themselves up to their eyes as a disguise, but now I was sure it was only to keep warm.

"My own interest is the bassoon," said Nicky slowly, staring at Giovanna. "And when I thought of doing a series of concertos in period dress, I only thought of the bassoonists. But if the story expands to the whole *concept* of the musical schools of the *ospedali* . . . "

Without a glance at me, the two of them continued to wander closer to the altar. We would be here for a while.

The last time I'd been in the Pietà had been two nights ago, during the concert performance of *Orlando Furioso*. Gunther and Bitten had been sitting in front of me then, poor things. They'd quarreled soon after—what had they quarreled about? Had they told each other their family stories, and had Gunther somehow realized that he was also a descendent of Olivia Wulf? Had he wanted a share of the estate that Bitten planned to wrest away from Nicky? Had Bitten pushed him in the canal because of that? Was the overwhelming grief she exhibited now caused by guilt or remorse?

At least I knew one thing: Andrew was probably the bassoon thief. Albert's theory about Signore Sandretti's taking the bassoon for insurance purposes didn't hold water. The magazine clipping Albert had found in the bassoon clearly pointed to Andrew's involvement. It was the explanation that made the most emotional sense: Andrew and Nicky were rivals researching the Pietà music school. He'd wanted to get Nicky in trouble—serious criminal trouble—so that he'd have an open field for himself. And to an extent, he'd succeeded. Here was Nicky lurking about Venice incognito (as incognito as someone like her could ever be), while Andrew ensconced himself in the city for a year with the chief librarian of the Conservatory of Music at his beck and call. The camaraderie of musicians, indeed.

The sound of a violin being tuned up filled the church. Giovanna had taken her instrument from its case and the familiar notes of Vivaldi—any one of two hundred violin concertos—peeled forth. I looked up at the balcony and thought of a girl standing there, searching for her mother in the crowded congregation below. Andrew knew about being abandoned firsthand. On some level, many of us knew about it. We still wanted the mothers who'd rejected us.

Nicky made her way back to my pew and slid in beside me.

"So," I said. "Your film is going to be about the whole orchestra now, is it? Perhaps the plot now includes a love affair between the protégées of Vivaldi—a violinist and a bassoonist? I think the movie audience of the new millennium could handle that on screen."

"Umm, brilliant," said Nicky absently. "But I feel I'm going in the right direction now. Ever since I arrived in Venice last week, I've felt there were serious obstacles to my project. Namely Andrew. He may not be as fine a player as I am, but his credentials are better. He's a Ph.D.; he's a slogger, he's a fact-finder. While I'm more of a— visionary. When it comes down to it, Cassandra, I couldn't write a book about the Pietà, but I think I could produce a film. I know I could. The plot is coming together in my mind. I *see* it."

She gazed at Giovanna, bowing beautifully. "Isn't she divine? And her aunts! Such good cooks."

"Speaking of plots coming together. Speaking of Andrew," I said. "I didn't manage to tell you before dinner that I tracked down the missing bassoon." I told her about my visit to Graciela's antique shop with Albert. "Albert thinks it's Sandretti himself who stole the bassoon, for insurance reasons. Anyway, you'll have to go over there tomorrow and identify it. Then you can tell the police, get your passport back and go home to London."

"London?" Nicky said, as if she'd never heard of it.

"I don't think it was Sandretti, myself," I went on. "I suspect Andrew. I've suspected him all along. Albert found a magazine article of Andrew's stuffed in the bassoon. To my mind, that's proof."

"Other instruments, the piano and the violin for instance, have far greater tonal range. Yet what other instrument can alternate between bittersweet lyricism and outright jocularity with such engaging finesse?"

"That's it!"

"Load of codswallop. Andrew doesn't have the tiniest sense of humor. What does he know about lyricism or jocularity?"

"Then you know about the article?"

"I cleaned the mouthpiece with it. Must have slipped inside when I put it back together. If only I had that old bassoon here now. I'd love to play a duet with her."

The notes of the violin had gone all andante and Giovanna looked over at us—one of us—invitingly.

"I've been so lonely, Cassandra," said Nicky.

And I suddenly realized what she meant. She'd been lonely without music in the house. Lonely without Olivia to make music with. My moving down from the attic wasn't the solution at all. She thought she wanted company. She wanted another musician.

"The bassoon and the violin," Nicky said dreamily. "It's a perfect combination."

Seventeen

IT WAS NEARLY ELEVEN when we finally arrived at the restaurant just outside the old Ghetto walls. Tables had been placed outside, on the quay along the canal, and people passed in and out of the brightly lit restaurant with drinks and plates. The klezmer concert was taking place on a barge in the canal that had been secured to the quay. Giovanna jumped onto the barge and took out her violin. She played klezmer as well as she played Vivaldi. Nicky disappeared inside and reappeared with glasses of beer for us and a few "wee tit-bits," including plates of calamari and garlic-drenched shrimp.

The barge, rocking with drunken candles that spilled light onto the black water and against the high stone wall, was an extraordinary sight. The musicians, five of them with the addition of Giovanna, were in full swing. The soprano wail of Roberta's clarinet matched the machine-gun sweetness of Giovanna's violin. In a lower register throbbed the drum and bass. A saxophone came in and out of the conversation. Roberta wasn't holding back as she had the other night in the Piazza when she played jazz; now it was as if her breath existed only to come straight through the black and silver horn. Giovanna was right with her. Her bowing arm went like an automaton's; but the sounds were human—wrenching, delicious, delirious.

Above us the sky caught the musicians' electricity and tossed it around in the mysterious clouds. The klezmer music somersaulted in the street, bumped up the stone wall, swan-dived into the canal. Nicky was enthralled. Almost as much as playing herself, she loved to hear others perform. Corkscrews of her hair blew in the wind. She ate shrimp with one hand and beat the table with the other.

I hadn't noticed Francesca when we arrived, but after a few songs, I saw her standing on the bridge that led to the Campo di Ghetto Nuovo. Her hair was twisted up around her head; she was as lovely as a red-tipped lily. Though I could see she was leaning over the side of the bridge, caught up in the music Roberta made, I went toward her anyway.

"Good evening, Cassandra," she greeted me happily. When you were her age, it was enough to be finished with work for the day and out in the night with your dreams. "It was a slow day at the shop. I managed to work on my story." She patted her coat pocket from which a few pages protruded. "I would describe the story to you, but summaries of things often don't sound as well."

"Is it about music?"

"It's about love. That's all I can say."

"I'd like to read it."

"Not yet, not yet. But if I ever finish it, maybe you could translate it into English." She was almost flirtatious with me tonight. Perhaps it was only the giddiness of finishing a good paragraph.

"Maybe," I said. "I have so many projects, already." I pulled the two Latin American novels out of my satchel. *Lovers and Virgins* balanced on the railing like a bloated sacrificial lamb, while *Bashō in*

Lima was as austerely thin as an Asian ascetic. The music weaving around us had so much more vibrancy than either of these two books. "I can't decide which one to translate. I don't care much for either of them, but I don't know why."

"What should a novel have for you to wish to translate it?" asked Francesca.

I started to list some of what I considered to be the attributes of good fiction: transporting liveliness, sheer glory in language, characters with heart, and a mingled sense of life's majesty and terror, its silliness and joy. But it came to me that these qualities were only important to me when I read a book. I could happily translate a second-rate novel if I cared about it, if it became, in some way, *mine*.

"I can't quite explain," I said, now filled with wonder at the simplicity of it. "When I translate a book, it must become *my* book for the time I'm working on it. So I suppose what draws me to a book is some glimmer of whether it could become mine."

"But how can that be?" asked Francesca. "It's the author's. The author wrote it. It can never become yours."

"No, you're wrong in that," I said. "It becomes mine while I'm working on it. It becomes my English book, for it's my English that makes it."

"Translation is just substitution," Francesca said, but a little uncertainly. "You find an English word for my Italian word—that's all, isn't it?"

"In basic translation, yes, perhaps, but not when it has to do with literature. I must read the text and have the feeling and then describe the feeling. I can't have the feeling in Italian; I must have it in the middle of the two languages, but be able to describe it in English."

"Now I'm confused."

"Say in Italian, *I'm in love*." She did so. "Now feel it." She blushed.

I took her hand. "Now say, *I'm in love* in English." She said, *I am in love* with a charming accent, but then pulled away, disturbed as well as flattered. Her eyes rested on Roberta.

"I think I understand a little better now what you mean . . . about translation," she said. "You know, Roberta and I were speaking this evening about how glad we are to have met you, and Nicola too. Because you are so much older than we are, you can be our role models. I said to Roberta, 'It is as if they are our mothers, but so much better, so much more wise and understanding.'"

"Thank you," I said weakly. "I'll pass that on to Nicky."

Francesca touched my arm and then walked over the bridge down to the quay where she joined Nicky. The two of them waved at me, and Nicky laughed. I didn't think that Francesca had yet paid her the compliment of admiring her elderly wisdom.

I took off my beret and let the wind blow through my hair. No need to cover the gray now. I regarded my two books. At least I'd finally defined the trouble. Neither of them was mine; neither of them would ever become mine. It was as simple as that. It was useless to debate the question of which one I should translate. The answer was neither.

I gave a push to *Lovers and Virgins*. The book fell like a stone and sank without a murmur, with hardly a splash. *Bashō in Lima* gave a wistful flutter as it sailed down toward the canal. This book didn't sink, but rested lightly on the surface of the dark water like a seagull preening its feathers. Then the current took the little volume and carried it under the bridge. I rushed to the other side to see it. *Bashō* was taking passage through the wind-rippled surface of the canal, as if she had a destination in mind, as if she thought it necessary to visit the lagoon. She was a pilgrim of a book, no doubt about it.

❧

"One might think," said Anna de Hoog, suddenly appearing at my side on the bridge, "that we were watching a concert by the girls of one of the *ospedali*."

"If they'd been allowed to set foot outside the Pietà," I said. "If they'd been allowed to come to the Ghetto. If the Jewish girls had been allowed to play music like the Christians. If. If. If."

Anna smiled. She seemed slightly out of breath. She was still wearing jeans, and a tweed jacket that made her look bulkier around the torso. Running shoes too. She seemed ready for action tonight. Had she run all the way over here?

"I gather you got the note I left with Marco," I said. "I wanted to ask you . . ."

"Shhh . . ." she said, taking my arm. "Don't spoil the mood. All in good time I'll answer your questions. If I can." The sky above threw off darts of light. The storm was almost upon us.

Down below, on the barge, Nicky had joined the klezmer group. The saxophonist stepped off for a break, and Nicky took up another clarinet that Roberta had brought along. In her student days Nicky had played the clarinet in a local jazz group, there being no great demand for bassoonists in university pubs. She was rusty, I suppose, but not to me. She caught the notes Roberta tossed her and played with them like a kitten plays with a mouse. She stayed with Roberta as long as she could and then let Roberta go, a kite in the wind. The notes flew up and lost themselves in the crackling fizz of the approaching storm.

"It's extraordinary, when you think of it," Anna said. "That Venice was the one place in the world, in human history perhaps, where women were not just allowed to perform as musicians in public but were encouraged to be virtuosos. Where there was even a cult around them. Where listeners came from all over Europe just to hear them."

"They played, but they didn't compose," I said. "That's why we don't know their individual names. We have to call them *the girls.*"

"I don't believe they didn't compose," said Anna. "It's true they were not employed to write music, but I am sure that some of them composed. You don't stop doing what you are meant to, just because someone tells you not to."

"That's an optimistic view of history."

"It's an alternative view. It sees more value in the rebel than in the mainstream."

Gradually she had steered me off the bridge into the campo of the Ghetto. The music was fainter here, the thunder louder. We began to walk around the square.

"Rebels don't create an oeuvre," I said. "Marginalized and subject peoples don't leave records, or if they do, the records are destroyed."

"History is a matter of losing and finding, and knowing where to look," said Anna. "Hildegard von Bingen was only a name for many centuries, but now her work is performed everywhere. Even Vivaldi's music was more or less lost for two hundred years. There could well be great work by women composers in the archives. The *New Grove Dictionary of Women Composers* lists a dozen Venetian musicians, most from the Pietà. In fifty years, scholars may have restored to us their compositions."

The buildings around us had taken on an air of insubstantiality in the thunderous night. Generations of Jews had lived and died here. How could Anna speak so confidently of losing and finding when so many lives had been lost and would never be found again? The victors have always been very good at erasing all trace of those they've destroyed.

Never as much as tonight had I felt Venice's peculiar combination of enclosure and openness. The violent sky was huge, and the lagoon we were sinking into was almost as vast. But the city was folded and twisted in on itself like a crumpled set of ancient, now unreadable instructions.

We stood in a patch of space, open to the sky, while all around us meaning—alternative, received, rejected and recovered—multiplied like the bricks of houses fallen and rebuilt.

Anna put her arm around me, carefully, but gently pushed my hand away from her shoulder, as if guarding a wound. "Of course, to me," she said, "the thrill is in the pursuit. I don't like to find what I'm looking for too easily."

I almost said, "I won't make it too easy then," but realized she wasn't talking about me at all.

"When I first saw you on the bridge," she went on. "I thought you were Nicola. With your hair blowing and the cape—it makes you look bigger than you are. It made a very dramatic picture. Then I realized that Nicola was playing in the band. I hope she's safe with them. In some ways it might have been better if she could have kept hidden."

"Nicky is one of those historical cases for whom hiding is not really an option, not for long anyway."

At that moment the storm blasted down on us, as if Jehovah himself were punishing us for questioning his old male world order. Thunder rippled out in waves as lightning shredded the sky. But even through the deluge it was possible to hear screams coming from the direction of the quay and the barge.

Anna immediately dropped her arm from my waist and ran back the way we'd come. She ran holding her chest, and I realized with a start that she was probably wearing a shoulder holster.

What was she expecting to happen? Was Nicky really in danger? I ran after Anna as fast as I could. My hip complained bitterly.

When I reached the bridge, I saw that the barge had been untied

156

or cut loose from its moorings, and that a few people were scrambling to hold onto it. Otherwise the quay was empty, the crowd having scattered for shelter.

I stood on the bridge, my cloak flapping in the wind. I couldn't see Anna, I couldn't see Nicky. I couldn't see much of anything actually. I came down the steps of the bridge and, clutching my cape, moved to the shelter of the buildings as I made my way along the quay. The rain shattered against my skin. I felt like I was at the mercy of an out-of-control rain-making machine in a movie version of *Wuthering Heights*. Now for the close-up of my cloak blowing in the wind, my tear-stained, tormented look of loss: *Cathy!*

As I passed a doorway, someone pulled me in to the recess, not by my arm, but by my neck.

Eighteen

IT'S NOT PLEASANT to be strangled, even by something as innocuous as a necktie. Especially in the driving rain at night. No one could see me in the doorway, no one could help me but myself. I flung out my arms and tried to get a grip on the person behind me; I tried to kick; I tried to make some sound, any sound.

Not even a whisper came out. I could feel my eyes bulge, my hair spring into even denser curls. The black velvet cape grew heavier. My knees buckled and I thought I was losing consciousness, but it was that the strangler's hands had been forcibly detached from my neck by even more forcible hands. When my assailant let go, there was nothing to hold me up.

There was no fighting of the fists or knives variety, only grunts and scrabbling. My would-be murderer dashed off into the black downpour, and I turned to face Anna de Hoog who held a necktie in her hands.

For a few seconds I couldn't speak to thank her. Then I managed to croak, "It's a good thing you'd changed out of that skirt into jeans."

"Oh, I can do equally well in a skirt," she said imperturbably. "I have a black belt in karate. Did you see who it was?"

"No. He or she came up behind me."

"It was a he, I believe, by his smell and his necktie. Not terribly tall. Young. Wiry. He had a mask on, not a Venetian one, I might add. A ski mask."

"Marco?" I said. "But he should be with Frigga."

"We mustn't assume it was anyone we know. It could have been an impersonal robbery attempt."

I felt my neck. "It didn't seem very impersonal."

"Do you know why anyone would have been trying to hurt you? Do you think he might have believed you were someone else, like Nicola?"

"I don't know." I could hardly hear myself think for the thunder above and the rattle of rain on the stones. It hissed into the canal like tiny, hot glass pebbles. The barge, empty now and retied to the dock, bobbed with the misery of abandonment; the audience had scattered. Nicky and the others were nowhere in sight. The plates and wine glasses left on the quayside tables were as ghostly as the remains of an underwater banquet.

"Shall we find a quieter place to talk?" Anna asked. She resourcefully whipped out a small packet, unfurled a clear plastic poncho and placed it carefully over my head. That gave her fingers a quick chance to assess the state of my neck. Satisfied, she unfolded her own poncho and led me in the direction of the train station to a small bar. In the midst of the tourist trade, it seemed to have few pretensions. We took our drinks, me a Jamesons and Anna a Belgian beer, to one of two tables in the back.

The whisky helped my throat but didn't make the recent events seem any clearer. Anna sipped thoughtfully at her beer. She wasn't a beauty, but I wasn't sure why I'd ever thought her drab. Her eyes were intelligent, her mouth decisive and sensual.

"Anna," I said. "Just who are you? Who are you working for?"

She must have realized I would not accept the same old story about being an oboe player. "I'm afraid it's rather complicated," she said.

"Try me."

"Not yet, Cassandra."

"Don't you trust me?"

"In my line of work, trust is not a word we often use. I *like* you, Cassandra. Very much. But I suspected from the beginning you would be a complicating factor."

"Is that why you called me in London and told me there was no reason to come to Venice?"

She just smiled.

"But if it weren't for me and Albert, the bassoon wouldn't have been found."

"Then Albert still has it?" she murmured.

"In a manner of speaking." I pressed my lips together. Anna had been lightly stroking my arm. No, it would take more than that to make me crack.

I added, "I still don't know who stole it in the first place."

Anna took another small sip of her beer. "I think I can tell you that," she said. "I don't think there's any harm if I tell you that. It was Bitten."

"So it wasn't an insurance scam by Sandretti," I said. "How did you get the truth out of Bitten?"

"I decided to take Bitten and Andrew to an unfamiliar setting," she said. "To break them. I mean, to break their alibis, as you say."

She had increased her pressure on my arm. I was all too familiar with her breaking techniques. They gave me a tingle even now.

"I persuaded them to make an excursion with me to the cemetery island to see the graves of Stravinsky and Wagner. Then I got Andrew off alone for a bit to discuss woodwind technique."

"Andrew must have forgiven you your oboe playing," I observed.

"Praise, especially if sincere, is often a useful thing. I admitted very frankly to Andrew that I was out of my depth among such a distinguished group of musicians. That I particularly wished to single him out as he was the best bassoonist of them all. That I had much to learn from him musically and that I was fascinated by his scholarship."

"And he believed every word you said."

"Why shouldn't he? It agreed with what he believes—what he would like to believe—about himself."

"Then, let me guess, at some point you slipped the conversation around to the evening of Gunther's death, and you got him to tell you what he overheard of Bitten's and Gunther's quarrel."

"You do not lack a logical mind, Cassandra Reilly."

"Well? What were Gunther and Bitten fighting about?"

"The bassoon, of course. Gunther had deduced that it was Bitten who had taken it, and he was urging her to acknowledge that she had, and that she'd recognized it in Albert's possession. When Andrew and Marco came up to Gunther and Bitten, they were standing near the naval museum. Bitten was saying, 'I am not going to say I took it. I didn't mean to. It was just that she made me so angry. I didn't think it would turn out like this.'

"But instead of being sympathetic, Gunther was upset and disappointed, and when he saw Marco and Andrew, he simply turned and walked away. Then Bitten rushed past them, in the direction of the Pietà."

"She must have gone to the Danieli, to try to get the bassoon at the left luggage," I said. "Marco turned up there a while later. As you did yourself. All of you inquiring about the bassoon."

"And you know this, how?"

"From he who placed the bassoon there in the first place with instructions to be told who asked about it."

"Your friend Albert is a clever fellow," Anna said, but she looked a little annoyed. "Nor did I realize that Marco had asked about it."

"Well, it makes sense, doesn't it? Marco and Andrew went for a drink at the Danieli. Marco was worried about the bassoon. He thought, from what Albert had said, that the bassoon was in the left luggage."

"Andrew told me that he and Marco were at the Danieli bar," said Anna. "But I did not realize that either of them was at any point alone."

"If you can call it being alone in a big hotel like that with snobbish receptionists watching your every move," I said, still smarting from my encounter with the desk clerk. "Anyway, are you going to tell me why Bitten took the bassoon and what she did with it?"

"Are you going to tell me where the bassoon is now?" she countered.

"Are you going to tell me what your role in all this is?"

"No," she smiled. She looked up, and I thought she was going to suggest another drink, something I felt, frankly, I could enjoy. "The rain seems to be less. I will tell you about my conversation with Bitten on the way back to the *palazzo*."

"You want to go back out into that weather? It's not less. I mean, it's still raining quite hard."

"Yes, I'm sorry, but I'm a bit tired, Cassandra."

She didn't seem tired; she seemed impatient, as if she'd remembered someone or something at the *palazzo* she needed to see.

A little grumpily, I followed her to the nearest *vaporetto* stop, and we found seats in the covered part of the boat. Through the steamy windows, the palaces along the canal were a blur of light.

Her face reflected the particular wet melancholy of Venice. Melancholy, but romantic. I thought of the two books lying together at the bottom of a murky canal. Would they ever find each other, or were they just too different?

I thought she was going to whisper, "Let's drop this whole thing and spend the night wandering the streets and waterways. I want to hear your life story, Cassandra, and what brought you to this city on the edge of the Adriatic. I want to share myself with you."

Instead she said, "I promised to tell you about Bitten."

"Umm."

"After we found Stravinsky's grave, I walked alone with her a short while. She refused to discuss what had happened to Gunther, but she seemed very sad, of course, being in the cemetery. I took advantage of this, I'm afraid, and kept leading the conversation back to how this whole situation began. It was in this way that I heard of her belief that she is the granddaughter of Olivia Wulf. I heard of her conflict with Nicola. I heard of her dislike of Nicola. It was a short step from that to suggest, sympathetically of course, that perhaps she had taken the bassoon in order to punish Miss Gibbons. At first she denied it, but when we were joined by Andrew, she had to confess. He said to Bitten, 'Look, I've told Anna what I overheard of your quarrel with Gunther. You admitted to him you took the bassoon. Now's your chance to make it all right.' Canadians are so very honest, don't you think?"

"Perhaps," I said.

"At any rate, Bitten finally admitted she'd been so annoyed at Nicola that she simply let herself into the room while Nicola was napping that afternoon and took the bassoon. Bitten says the room was not locked; Nicky says it was. That is something we can't prove, and it's of little importance."

"What did Bitten do with the bassoon then? They had a concert that evening, and she knew Nicky would discover the theft very quickly."

"Bitten hadn't quite thought that out. First she went to the train station to hide it in a locker, but the bassoon did not fit. To hand such an oddly shaped parcel to the men at the left luggage department would have given them a chance to identify her later. She was already starting to feel uncomfortably conspicuous. She was afraid someone might think the bassoon was a gun. She did not think of selling it, nor did she want to destroy it. She wanted only to get Nicola in a spot of trouble. Bitten told me she even fantasized she might come to the 'rescue' of Nicola and that Nicola would be grateful to Bitten instead of so hostile."

"Fat chance," I said. "But I get the picture. Bitten was panicking. She didn't have much time."

"That's correct. She wanted to be back before Nicky discovered that the bassoon was gone. Finally she became desperate. She found a gondola that was unattended and placed the parcel under the seat. She imagined that when the gondolier returned and found the package, it would be turned over to some sort of Lost and Found Department. In Sweden it would have been."

"But, in fact," I said, as the *vaporetto* approached Accademia, "the gondolier found it and gave it to his brother, who ran an antique store, and that was how Albert's friend Graciela was able to track it down for him. But why did Sandretti say he didn't recognize it? Why did Marco and Bitten go along with him?"

Anna was through sharing confidences. "The important thing," she said, "is to get the bassoon back. You have the address of this woman, Graciela? I must speak to her."

"Not so fast, Miss de Hoog," I said. "My primary aim is to make sure Nicky gets out of this without a stain on her reputation."

As the *vaporetto* tied up at the dock, Anna jumped out. She seemed more than impatient now, anxious even. I followed more slowly. "I have been meaning to ask you," she said, rather brusquely, "Are you crippled?"

"No. I had a close encounter recently with some turtle eggs in the South Pacific."

"I suggest we part here," she said abruptly. "Your hotel is this way, and the *palazzo* is this way." She gave me a quick buffeting that I couldn't interpret and dashed off.

No, I wasn't going back to my hotel, not yet. Something must be happening at the Sandrettis'. But what and how would Anna know? Or did she just not want someone—who?—to see us together?

When I arrived at the *palazzo* five minutes after Anna, I had to wait almost as long for someone to answer the door bell. Finally Bitten came to the door. She was wearing a white terry-cloth robe that had "Hotel Danieli" stitched over one breast, and her feet were bare.

"What's happened?" I said.

She motioned up the stairs. "There's been a break-in tonight. In Sandretti's library."

Nineteen

GRAY IS NOT A COLOR one immediately associates with opulence. When the library door was open briefly a few days before, I had been puzzled by an impression of something leaden about the grandeur within. Now I followed Bitten up the stairs into the room and discovered the reason. The ceiling and wall decorations were done entirely in *grisaille*, a technique of painting in tints of gray to suggest the bas-reliefs of classical sculpture, and this soft grayness enfolded the room like fur, lending a smoky cast to all that was not painted. Vast bookshelves covered much of two walls. On a third wall a Baroque marble fireplace and mantle carved with nymphs was flanked by tall windows, draped in silvery-blue velvet. Tiers of ancient musical instruments arrayed the fourth wall. In the center of the room was a huge globe so darkened by time that the continents swam in shadow. Heavy, cracked-leather chairs with clawed feet sat next to the fireplace. On one of these chairs, Andrew reclined, looking, in his pajamas, like a sleepy little boy.

There were touches of gaiety. The mural over the mantle showed

Venetian ladies in frothy petticoats attended by aroused satyrs, and the decorations were full of pretty girls and cupids, but all was gray, as if in a dream without color. The carpet underfoot was like a layer of blue-gray dust, but on top of its lightness squatted heavy book-shelves and furniture. Nothing could be heavier than the massive carved desk around which Sandretti, Marco and Anna stood, in a curious sort of intimacy.

The desk's drawers hung open, their contents scattered over the floor. The papers on top were in disarray. Sandretti, in formal evening wear, looked more annoyed than frightened. Marco stood next to him, and it was easy to see their close resemblance, though Marco had a helpless expression. Only Anna looked competent to deal with whatever had happened, but her mouth was set. Was this all part of her plan, or was she dismayed by a new turn of events? I couldn't tell.

I asked, "Have you called the police?"

All three of them, Sandretti, Marco and Anna, said no. "Si-gnore Sandretti does not believe that anything has been taken from his desk," Anna said shortly.

Anna circled in on Andrew, who shrank into his chair. His pa-jamas were navy blue flannel, dark against his freckled white skin. "And none of you heard anything?"

"I'd just gone to sleep," said Andrew, pouting a little in the di-rection of Marco. It was clear he'd been hoping to be joined in bed, but hadn't been.

"I was in the bath," said Bitten. "Suddenly I heard shouting. I got up and came to see. The Signore was shouting at Marco."

"I fell asleep," said Marco miserably. "I came into the library to read a book, and I fell asleep. Someone came in while I was sleeping and did this. I feel very, very guilty. My father is right to be angry."

Anna didn't look as if she believed him. Had she seen, as I had, the scrapes around the lock that suggested a forcible entry?

Frigga came into the library. "What is it?" she asked in German.

"It is nothing," Anna replied. "Marco fell asleep and someone came into the library and mussed the desk."

Frigga turned to Marco and said in English. "I asked you to bring me some warm milk, young man. But you did not."

"When was that?" asked Anna.

Frigga looked at her watch. "More than an hour ago. I have been waiting!"

Which meant the person who tried to strangle me couldn't have been Marco. I glanced at Anna, but she ignored me.

"I am sorry," said Marco. "I mean to bring you the milk. But I fell asleep."

Sandretti had said nothing through all this, but now he lashed out at his son with invective.

Andrew tried to intervene. "The important thing is that nothing was taken."

But Anna was looking at the tiers of instruments displayed on the wall above the desk. "When I was last here," she said conversationally, "there were two violins in the middle row. But now I believe there is only one."

Sandretti boxed his son's ears, and Marco cowered.

Andrew leapt up, but Bitten pulled him back.

Frigga looked bewildered, Anna thoughtful.

What I wanted to know was, where did Bitten get that bathrobe?

"We shall search the house," said Sandretti.

"The morning is time enough to call the police and report the theft," said Anna in a low voice to Sandretti. And then to the rest of us, she said, "It's after midnight. I personally am off to bed." She did not look at me as she went by. Her leaving seemed to drain the room of drama, and the others mumbled that they too would go to their rooms and deal with this tomorrow. Marco was the first to leave, fleeing his father, and Andrew went after him. Bitten turned to Frigga and for the first time seemed to see her as she was, a frail figure in a foreign country. She took Frigga's arm and slowly led her from the library.

This left only Sandretti at the desk, head in his hands, not making any attempt to straighten the mess. I pitied him, and yet there was some hint of an elaborate play about the incident that troubled me. The theft might have been real, but it was not completely unexpected.

I returned to my hotel, vowing I would wash my hands of the whole affair.

When I woke up the next morning, I reached automatically for *Lovers and Virgins*, but it wasn't there. I recalled again how fast the novel had sunk, like an accused witch during the Inquisition. I felt lost, but also free. Free to lie here in my soft hotel bed, at liberty to listen to the rain falling heavily against the windows. I didn't have to move, I could order breakfast in bed.

I didn't have to read; I could just lie here, imagining the last hundred pages of the Venezuelan novel.

Lourdes would rise to the rank of Mother Superior of the order and become a patron saint of the poor and visionary (the author had clearly had her headed for the insane asylum, but I wasn't having any of that).

Mercedes would write a great feminist tract that would result in her being excommunicated. She would flee to Paris, where she'd spend her remaining years attending the salons of Madame de Staël and perhaps befriending Mary Wollstonecraft. (Instead of becoming a strange and embittered spinster recluse.)

I suspected the author had had plans to marry off both Maria and Isabella. Fine—let Maria's stable hand turn out to have escaped the fire, and let him and Maria find each other again in middle age on the Technicolor pampas. But Isabella—who was good enough for her? Perhaps the eldest daughter of the neighboring *hacienda*. Let them discover happiness together, merge their property and start a school for the children of their workers.

I basked a little in alternatives I'd just bestowed upon these imaginary characters. I was giving them something better, these poor slaves of fiction who had otherwise been force-marched under armed guard, with shackles on their wrists and ankles, along the dusty roads of the author's weak imagination.

I basked, and then I sighed. I got up and brought over to the bed the pile of second-string novels, the other three books that Simon had asked me to look at. Unless I wanted to depend on Nicky's hospitality the whole winter, I would have to find something here to translate, something that I could stomach translating and that, unlike poor *Bashō in Lima,* had more print than white space.

But before I could investigate them further, there was a knock on my door. Hastily pulling on a pair of black jeans, I went to open it, expecting that Anna de Hoog might have had a change of heart and was here to tell me whom she was working for and why.

It was Roberta, in a heavy slicker and tall green gum boots, carrying a large plastic carrier bag.

"The water is rising," Roberta said, throwing off her slicker and shaking her curly black head. "It's the *acqua alta,* the high tide. In another hour, many low-lying passageways will be flooded and difficult to get through."

As she took off her boots, there was another knock. Who now? But it was only the maid, with coffee and croissants.

"I took the liberty of ordering breakfast," said Roberta. "I have something to show you. She pulled a paper-wrapped parcel from her carrier and began to unwrap its contents.

"You left the restaurant very suddenly last night," I said. "The rain started, the barge sailed off, and you were nowhere to be seen." I almost added, "and someone tried to choke me," but I didn't want to appear melodramatic.

"I saw my brother there last night, and I knew that if he was there, then I could get into my father's house. When the rain started, I ran off."

"Your brother?" I said, gulping coffee. "Your brother was at the restaurant? But Frigga says she saw him at the *palazzo*; she asked him to bring her a glass of milk, and *he* says he slept right through the break-in."

As Roberta unwrapped the last of the parcel, I suddenly realized I didn't need to tell her that her father's library had been robbed.

There lay the evidence, in the form of two leather-bound volumes much like the one we'd seen yesterday in the conservatory library. Instead of Anna Maria stamped in gold, the name was Vittoria Brunelli.

"Vittoria Brunelli was from my mother's side of the family," explained Roberta excitedly. "I suppose the bassoon belonged to her once. We can probably look back in the records of the Pietà and find that she was in the *figlie del coro*. But look!" She opened one of the volumes. "This is Vivaldi, I believe—the scores of his bassoon concertos. But the other book has music that I don't recognize as Vivaldi's. Of course it could be some other composer, but what if it is her own music? I believe it might be, because of this."

Roberta took a letter that had been folded twice from the back of the volume.

"It seems to be to some member of her family, probably a brother or sister, given the manner of address. It's dated 1746, and she is writing from the Pietà. You know they also taught music to talented girls from good families who were not orphans; she must have been one of them. She is talking about several recent performances, at least one of which featured a concerto of her own. Earlier Vittoria had composed in Vivaldi's style; now, she writes, 'The bassoon concerto was in my own hand, written in secret,' and goes on:

You must understand that I could not do otherwise. They would not take me seriously; they would never let me compose. The music of others is like words addressed to me: I must answer and hear the sound of my own voice. And the more I hear that voice, the more I realize that the songs and sounds which are mine are different."

"But this is exactly what Nicky has been looking for," I exclaimed. "A woman from the Pietà who composed her own music. A bassoonist, no less. What if some of those thirty-nine bassoon concertos are hers? And to think, it was in your father's library all this time."

"I should have put it together sooner," Roberta said. "But I have never known a great deal about my mother's family. My mother died when I was eight. My father, of course, had a collection of instruments when I was growing up. I always remember him claiming that several came from the *ospedali*, but I never realized that the instruments were part of my mother's dowry and that there might be more than just instruments. When I saw the leather-bound volume of Anna Maria in the library of the conservatory, I remembered similar volumes I'd seen and been curious about as a child."

"You didn't ransack your father's desk then?"

"I didn't touch his desk! I went right to the shelves and found these where I remembered them. It took only about ten minutes altogether. When I returned home, I discovered the letter inside. There may be others there in the library."

"Did anyone see you?"

"The old German woman stuck her head out the door as I was leaving, and asked me something in German, so I just nodded and said, *Si, si, signora.*"

"She thought you were Marco and were going to bring her some milk, poor thing. She must not have realized she was speaking in German. Did you lock the library door as you left?"

"No. I'd forced it open and had broken the lock. I still had a key to the house, but not to the library. When I was growing up, the library was never locked."

"So someone must have come in after you, looking for something different. Andrew and Bitten were back from the cemetery. Anna de Hoog was gone . . . it couldn't have been Frigga?"

Roberta shrugged. "Was anything taken?"

"Yes, a violin."

"My father's financial situation is very poor. He has many expenses and appearances to live up to. But I don't think he makes much money from arranging concerts. He used to have my mother's money, but he spent it. I suppose he is trying to steal the instruments from himself to collect insurance. First the bassoon and now this violin."

"But he didn't steal the bassoon," I said, and gave her the background. I was puzzled, to say the least, by Signore Sandretti. Every time I'd seen him, he had seemed to be in a foul mood, which had been directed mainly at Marco.

"My father has a very bad temper," Roberta agreed. "He often beat us when we were growing up. When he found out I was a lesbian, he made me leave home."

"When was that?"

"About five years ago when I was twenty. I was glad to go, to tell you the truth. I don't like my brother, but I feel sorry for him, living with our father. Whether or not he is gay, he should be treated better. It has bred a kind of hatred in Marco for our father, a desire to punish him, and yet Marco still feels that our father will protect him. Francesca's mother is not very happy about our relationship, but she would never make her leave home. Well, perhaps that would be better. We could live together."

For Roberta and Francesca, I saw, living together was a beautifully romantic prospect. Far be it from me to suggest otherwise. Personally I ran from the thought of a domestic relationship based on the instability of romance. Nicky and I wouldn't have survived all these years together if we'd been in love.

"It will work out," I said. "If nothing else, eventually your father will grow old and lose his power over Marco. And over you."

"My father won't be old for years and years," said Roberta. She sighed and ran a hand through her black curls. Centuries before, like her relative Vittoria Brunelli, Roberta probably would have grown up in a convent or been turned over to the Pietà when her mother died. I pictured her in a severe dress with a little lace at her collar. It wouldn't have suited her as well as jeans.

"Come on," I said, "I know Nicky would like to see these volumes of music. She'll be over the moon about them, in fact." It struck me that I hadn't seen Nicky since last night. She didn't even know that someone had tried to strangle me.

"If you don't have boots," said Roberta, "you might want to put these plastic bags over your shoes."

I laughed. I might not have a fabulous fashion sense, but no way was I going to walk around Venice with plastic bags on my feet. It didn't make it any better that I didn't have my usual leather jacket, but instead had to wear the flowing black velvet cloak, now sadly bedraggled around the edges.

I changed my mind about footwear when we got downstairs to the lobby. Water was just beginning to slosh over the threshold onto the marble floor of the entry hall. The management had installed two planks as well as a woman with a mop. Outside, the Záttere was flooded. It was as if the Giudecca Canal came right up to the buildings. Rain gushed down; everything was a gray-white blur.

I stepped back inside and put the heavy plastic bags Roberta offered over my shoes. Then we began to make our way through the streets of the Dorsoduro to Nicky's hotel. Wooden platforms lay end to end like low banquet tables over some of the streets. Two opposing streams of people snaked along the platforms above the water. Their feet made a rumbling sound, off-stage thunder at a provincial theater. In front of the Accademia, lines of tourists under umbrellas huddled miserably.

As we came closer to the twisted passageways around the Frari, it got worse. There were no platforms, and the water was often up to mid-calf. Finally we reached the hotel and climbed onto the dry land that was the tiny lobby. Upstairs, I knocked twice at Nicky's door.

There was no answer, but I heard movement inside.

"Nicky, it's me. And Roberta. We have something to show you."

Now I heard whispering. Giovanna was certainly there with her. All the better.

"Go away, Cassandra. Come back later. This is not a convenient time."

"Open up," I repeated. "You wanted a Pietà bassoonist," I said. "Well, I've brought you one."

Twenty

WITHIN A FEW MINUTES, Nicky, Giovanna and Roberta were piled on the bed examining the bound music of Vivaldi and Vittoria Brunelli. It reminded me of how my sisters used to heap themselves up like kittens to look first at comic books and then *Secret Romance*. I'd never joined them, feeling myself too different. It was the same now. I perched on a chair and watched Nicky and Giovanna exclaim over Roberta's find (though *steal* seemed a better description than *find*). They'd already been looking through the volume of violin music belonging to Anna Maria, the *maestra*. Notes for a narrative lay scattered about the bed. Although I'd never be a musician like them, I was happy to realize that the girls in the *ospedali* were no longer faceless orphans. They had names now—Vittoria Brunelli, Anna Maria. They were about to enter recorded history again, after a long absence. They had families again.

I interrupted Nicky once to give her Graciela's shop address and to tell her that the sooner she got there to identify the bassoon, the sooner she'd be in the clear. "Anna told me last night it was Bitten who took the bassoon, as you suspected, and for the very obvious reasons. I suppose you could get someone to press charges, but it might be better just to let it go."

"Oh, but we'll need the bassoon for our film," said Nicky, and I had the feeling she did not intend to let the instrument be given back to Signore Sandretti. So perhaps she would become a bassoon thief after all.

"Bitten?" said Giovanna. "Is she the one who lost her lover?"

"The woman who wants my house and everything in it," said Nicky, but she didn't seem, at least at the moment, particularly perturbed. She lay in splendor, curls abundant, red dressing gown open to her powerful chest.

"She could be a consultant on the film," said Giovanna, "that might make her happy."

"She bloody well . . ." began Nicky, but Giovanna stopped her lips with a finger. "I am going to be the Italian producer," she told me. "When my term ends in November, Nicky and I will go to Rome for two weeks and then back to London. I suppose I'll see you there."

Roberta was looking at them in fascination. Now, at last, she had some true role models. "Perhaps Francesca and I will visit London during Christmas season too."

"The house is big enough for everyone," I said. The idea of music again in the rooms below my attic filled me with pleasure.

I picked up my leather jacket from among the clothes on the floor and put it on. I straightened my beret. My character is such that when I have a mind to go, I go. I have made rapid and unpremeditated departures from all sorts of places, and all sorts of situations. Nicky is used to it. She understood, when I got up from the bed where the three of them were happily poring over Vittoria's bassoon concertos and plotting how they would do further research on her life, that when I said, "I'm off," I did not mean I was planning a visit to the Palace of the Doges, but that I had decided to go back to London.

"Cassandra," Nicky said, "I probably won't be back for a week or two, until I have the concert at the Purcell Room. Take care of the mail, will you? And everything?"

I kissed her full, soft cheek. "Thanks for the trip to Venice," I said. I decided not to tell her I'd almost been strangled on her account. Let bygones be bygones.

"Cassandra?" she said, her eyes filling, but I waved and went out the door.

My dear friend was far too sentimental sometimes.

I splashed back through the streets to my hotel room. It was hard going in places, but I felt strangely exhilarated, the way I always do when I am seriously on the move. It's true, major questions were still unanswered: Who had killed Gunther? Who, for that matter, had tried to kill me? Who'd taken the violin last night? Had I done anything to help or just confused things more? I might just stop by the Sandretti *palazzo* on my way to the Piazzale Roma. Something Roberta had said still echoed within me; her suspicion that her father had been stealing the instruments himself. Was Anna de Hoog working for him or against him?

I packed, put the three remaining Latin American books in my satchel and set off through the still-flooded streets, carrying my small suitcase above my head. The city was beautiful, but it was sinking. One of my plastic foot-bags had punctured, and an unpleasant wetness was creeping up one leg of my Levi's. I wanted to get to dry ground, wanted to get *off* the ground in fact. I'd go to the airport and just wait for the next flight back to London. All I had to do first was ask a few more questions.

178

This time Sandretti himself came to the door. I thought he had aged a great deal in the last few days; perhaps Roberta's fear that her father would never grow old was unfounded. His skin was gray, his eyes, hunted and guilty. He had obviously been about to go out in a hurry and seemed taken aback to see me there with my suitcase, even when I told him I wasn't staying, that I just wanted to make a few good-byes. He had clearly never placed me in the ménage of musicians, yet he wasn't sure I *wasn't* one of them either. He told me he believed Bitten was practicing and that Frigga had just returned from a last visit to the police. She would be flying back to Germany with Gunther's body this afternoon. His whole manner suggested that he wished I would go away and as soon as possible.

His nervousness only made me curious, and I eased my way around his solid body into the foyer to indicate I wasn't to be put off so easily.

"I'm just on the way to the airport myself," I said. "Of course I know that Nicky's not around—wonder whatever happened to her?—but what about Marco and Andrew?"

"Mr. McManus is moving to his permanent accommodations this morning. My son is assisting him." Sandretti averted his eyes. I wondered what this was all about. Marco couldn't be leaving home finally, could he? Especially not in the company of Andrew?

"Well, I'll just pop up and say good-bye to Frau Hausen," I said, pushing past him to get to the stairs. I refused to ask about Anna de Hoog. She'd hardly noticed when I left the *palazzo* last night. She was probably in cahoots with Sandretti anyway. Behind me the door closed; Sandretti had slipped out. Clearly, he didn't want to be here when the two boys arrived.

I went quickly up the stairs and knocked on Frigga's door. Across the *piano nobile* I could hear Bitten playing the mournful adagio again.

Frigga was sitting on her bed, with her back to the door, dressed in her Chanel suit, a hat and gloves. A dark raincoat lay half-folded neatly beside her. She was small and old and in great pain.

I sat as gently as I could beside her. "Frau Hausen, excuse me for troubling you, but what was the name of your son-in-law?"

"Jakob," she answered after a moment. "Jakob Wulf."

"Did you know his mother was a very famous musician, who got out of Austria and to London before the war?"

"My daughter said something about that. But she told me he and his mother had a terrible quarrel. His mother did not like the girl Jakob was going to marry."

"Not your daughter Dorothea?"

"No, another girl. I don't know her name. Elizabeth perhaps. But she was frightened when the war started. She and her mother went to Sweden where they had friends."

"And Jakob married Dorothea instead. . ." Now it was clear what had been troubling me in the conductor's biography. He had called Elizabeth Jakob's fiancée, not his wife. It had been the most obvious thing to assume they had gone ahead and married. "Do you have by chance a photograph of Jakob, Frau Hausen?"

"No," she said. "Not here. Why?"

"It's a long story, but Bitten's mother died recently in Sweden. Bitten had some reason to believe that her mother, Elizabeth, knew Jakob and his mother, Olivia Wulf. And that Bitten was Jakob's daughter. I've been trying to put together her story." I was relieved I wouldn't have to tell Bitten that she was Gunther's aunt.

"Bitten says she loved Gunther," Frigga said slowly. "How can that be, to fall in love so quickly? He would have told me, wouldn't he? He was my little boy. My last one."

She didn't cry; she sat very still, facing the window.

I went across to Bitten's room. The house was absolutely quiet except for her muted notes. I remembered what Nicky had said about the bassoon being used during musical settings in the underworld. I hesitated before knocking. Should I be the one to tell Bitten that her mother had been Jakob's fiancée, not his wife? That she had no claim to Olivia's name or estate?

I was glad for Nicky, of course, not just that she could keep the house, but that she wouldn't lose the sense that *she* and she alone had been Olivia's favorite. But everything else was terribly sad. Gunther's senseless death, Bitten's loss. Olivia would never know she'd had a great grandson. Perhaps what saddened me most was the story of Ruth, Gunther's mother, the talented violinist who had destroyed herself. No, history was not optimistic. History was not kind.

The adagio ended, with a sweet sorrowful flourish, but Bitten didn't go on to the allegro movement that would end the concerto, round it out and create wholeness. Instead, the mournful notes of the adagio began again. She would play them until she moved on, but I didn't have time to listen. I knocked, *con vivace*.

Bitten wasn't dressed; she was wearing the same Hotel Danieli terry-cloth robe. I said I was leaving, and had just come to say goodbye.

"I'm leaving too," she said. "I have a flight to Stockholm tonight. I play in a recital tomorrow. That is good. I need to begin my life again. Please tell Nicola . . ." But she stopped; she didn't know what to tell Nicola. I held my tongue. If Bitten did any sort of serious investigation, she would find out soon enough.

We shook hands. Then, just as she was closing the door, I said, as if it had just occurred to me, "Why do you have a bathrobe that says Hotel Danieli?"

She paused. "It . . . it isn't mine, it was Gunther's. He was staying here, but he had another room there. We used to go there . . . to be alone. We did not have enough privacy here."

Just as Bitten shut the door, Anna came out of her room, as if the two motions were attached. She had an oddly alert look that took me in but somehow did not quite see me. In fact, she pushed me down as I came toward her, pushed me right down in front of her, and drew her gun, and pointed it down the stairs. Andrew had just come in the front door, whistling something from *The Four Seasons*. Two plainclothes police, also with guns, appeared and had his arms behind his back before he could get to the end of "Spring."

Andrew! It all made sense now. He was the one who had killed Gunther and had tried to kill me. I had been taken in by his assertions of gay solidarity.

Anna rushed downstairs. There was a scramble, and everyone was shouting, Andrew loudest of all. "Marco," he was screaming. "Get away."

But it was too late. Anna de Hoog had flung herself on someone just outside the door and had his arms behind him in a fierce grip. When the rest of us got outside, he was handcuffed and lying on his side, and she was just returning her gun to her shoulder holster.

"I'm so glad he didn't run," she said, hardly winded and very pleased. "I really hate to shoot people."

"Is it for stealing the violin last night?" I asked. Andrew I could believe as a murderer, but not sweet little Marco. One of the Italian cops had bundled Andrew into a room in the *palazzo*, from whence we heard his anguished cries.

"You may take a good look now at the person who tried to kill you, Cassandra," Anna said. "And at the man who knocked Gunther on the head and pushed him into the canal from a hotel window."

Marco's beautiful face stared angrily up at us. He said to the

Italian policeman next to Anna de Hoog, "My father won't allow this. My father will have your job! Where is my father?"

But Marco was an orphan now. His father was nowhere in sight.

Twenty-one

"IT BEGAN SIMPLY," said Anna, from a recumbent position nearby. "I was assigned by Interpol to investigate a series of cases that involved antique musical instruments being stolen in Italy. The instruments came from private collections, from small or provincial libraries and from unguarded museums or churches. The name Sandretti had come up more than a few times. His wife had been wealthy, but he himself was only a sort of musical entrepreneur. He held prestigious positions that could not have paid terribly well, at least not well enough to allow him to live as well as he did. There are all sorts of men like that in Italy, you understand. Generally there are under-the-table arrangements going on, various pleasant schemes between friends to fill each other's pockets. Certainly nothing for Interpol."

She stroked my arm gently. It was early afternoon, and the rain was easing off. The luxurious hotel room was a little humid; from below, I could hear motorboat wash rippling through the canal and gondoliers singing to their passengers. Mostly O Sole Mio. Her gun in its shoulder holster lay on the pillow by her head. I hate to admit it had rather excited me.

"The thefts had been going on for years, but in the last year they had become more frequent and more noticeable. In the past, often what happened is that a lesser instrument would be substituted for a more valuable one. Perhaps they ran out of lesser instruments! At any rate, there began to be more daring robberies, from larger museums. The Italians called on us for help.

"I am one of the few agents with a background in music, though as I mentioned, trombone was more my specialty than Baroque woodwinds. I was able to persuade a young bassoonist to help in our investigation. In retrospect, I wish I had not. I wish I had carried out the investigation on my own. But it was thought that an inside source would be of great use, and it was unclear whether I could get myself invited to Venice for this symposium. We wanted to get into Sandretti's world, you see, and we understood that he often had musicians staying at his *palazzo*. I suppose it was another way of augmenting his income. He would pocket the funding that should have gone to pay for hotel rooms.

"Gunther agreed to be a sort of mole, to watch Sandretti unobtrusively and to see how he operated. It was through Gunther that I ended up being invited as well. Sandretti was a little surprised by me, but since he had so much respect for Gunther, he accepted my presence.

"We also set Gunther up here in this room in the Danieli, so that he would have another base, especially if anything went wrong. I can certainly take care of myself as you know, but he was an amateur. He entered right into the spirit of things, however, and decided himself on the code word he would use when calling me."

"Frigga!" I said, finding my voice for the first time in a while. I had been so filled with well-being up to now that I hadn't been quite paying attention.

"Yes. Things were going well until the moment that the bassoon was stolen. Although a stolen instrument is just what we were expecting, I hardly expected that it would go missing in such a public way or that it would be a bassoon belonging to Signore Sandretti himself. Although the bassoon certainly has historic value, it is hardly in the same league as the violins and cellos we'd been looking at. I was very puzzled at Sandretti's reaction too. He immediately accused Nicola of taking it, called in the police, had her passport confiscated. It seemed a great show of firmness.

"Interesting, I thought. Perhaps he is not the person we are looking for after all. All the same, his reaction was very strange. I didn't for a minute, of course, think that Nicola had stolen the bassoon, but I couldn't imagine that Sandretti had done it and blamed it on her. I was as intrigued as anyone when your friend Albert turned up with the bassoon and Sandretti said he'd never seen it before.

"Actually, your friend Albert threw me completely off the track for a while. I kept trying to figure out what role he was playing in all this—was he working for Sandretti or against him?—I didn't understand for a long while that it was as simple as it was: He was a casual acquaintance of yours and was doing you a favor, a favor that might involve some reward for himself.

"A great deal about Albert seemed mysterious, aside from those thin black gloves. But I did find out a few curious things about your Mr. Egg. His shop in Buxton is run without reproach by his elderly mother and specializes in antique tea sets, but Albert himself is frequently on the slightly shady side of the law. He travels a little more than he might, given the size of his shop and its contents, and he lives a little better than he might. He's too much of a small fry to investigate for theft or fraud, but there is a small file on him in England. Something you might mention to him if you have the opportunity."

I raised myself on my arm. My brain seemed to be working again, at least enough to know that I was puzzled. "But Sandretti didn't know that Bitten had taken the bassoon. Did he really think Nicky had done it? Or did he suspect his son and was he trying to protect him?"

"The latter, Cassandra. It was only last night that Sandretti gave up on his son. But let's go back a few days. Albert put the bassoon in the left luggage with instructions to his friend to keep an eye on it and tell no one it was there. Gunther was the first to leave the church during the performance of *Orlando Furioso*. He got a phone call, and Bitten followed soon after."

"Was it you who called him? How could you? You were playing in the orchestra."

"A colleague of mine rang Gunther on my instructions and told him to ask Bitten if it was she who had taken the bassoon. When Bitten admitted it was, they had a great quarrel, which Andrew and Marco observed. Bitten went back to the left luggage and tried to retrieve the bassoon but failed. She then went up to the hotel room in the Danieli, hoping Gunther would join her.

"Meanwhile Marco and Andrew had gone to the Danieli for a drink. Marco left Andrew in the bar and went to ask about the bassoon. At this point he observed Bitten, who had come downstairs to leave a message for Gunther at the desk. Marco discovered from the clerk that Gunther had a room at the hotel. Unfortunately, it had not occurred to him to register under a pseudonym.

"At this point Marco seems to have given way to terror. He had been feeling for a long while that he was under surveillance, and for some reason he picked up on Gunther right away. That was why you saw him following Gunther that morning in the *piazza*. At any rate he saw Gunther come into the Danieli and then go up the stairs. He followed him up and they had some kind of exchange. Marco hit

Gunther on the head and knocked him out. If only he had left then, everything would have been all right, for Gunther wasn't dead. But Marco, panic-struck, pushed him out the window into the canal. Marco rejoined Andrew at the bar, and they returned to the Pietà."

"And all Andrew remembered was that Marco gave him a kiss," I marveled.

"On closer questioning Andrew remembered that Marco had been gone a good twenty or thirty minutes."

Anna began gathering the underwear that was scattered around us on the king-size bed. She put on her shirt and checked that the trigger of her gun was on safety before slipping her arm through the holster.

Anna continued, "It was when I was at the left luggage asking about the bassoon that they found Gunther's body. I was quite shocked. I really couldn't believe that Sandretti had done it. He was not visible to the rest of you, but he was backstage the entire time, and I had a good view of him. Gunther's death made me rethink everything, and that is when I began to concentrate on Marco. Marco Sandretti had even less going for him than his father. He was young, he was not talented, he was dependent on his father. He had gotten involved in stealing instruments and smuggling and was desperate to conceal it. His father had guessed something like that was going on. He thought Marco had taken the bassoon. That's why he pretended the bassoon Albert recovered wasn't the bassoon that had been stolen."

I began slowly putting on my clothes. My plane was leaving in a few hours. The rain storm was over; the room was heating up. I hoped Anna would stop me from getting dressed, but she didn't. She'd already put on her shirt and jeans and was looking for her socks.

"Last night," she went on, "when Marco took the violin, Sandretti realized he couldn't go on covering up for him. He'd tried. He messed up the desk so it would look like someone was looking for money or papers and to draw attention away from the loss of the violin. But when I went back to the library after everyone had gone to sleep, he admitted he knew his son was involved in the thefts. I told him I thought Marco had killed Gunther and made an attempt on your life, and I wanted a chance to prove it. Sandretti agreed to stay out of the way this morning."

"But why did Marco try to strangle me? I thought he liked me."

"You must have done something to make him think you knew what he was up to."

I thought back. "Right before going to the klezmer concert I told Marco that I knew who had taken the bassoon and that the police would be making a thorough investigation. I also said the police would try to get to the bottom of his secrets, but that I'd never reveal them."

Anna looked at me with a half-smile. "And you're surprised he tried to shut you up?"

"I didn't think I was talking to a murderer! I was trying to cheer him up about his relationship with Andrew."

Anna was fully dressed now. She pushed her hair back off her face. I felt like saying something inane like: "Will I ever see you again?" but that was not my style. An intense feeling of *sabi* came over me. I tried to disguise it in pity for Andrew.

"I wonder if Andrew suspected Marco?"

"I think he must have," Anna said. "He was so distraught this morning. Now he says he's not going to stay in Venice. He says he can't stay here after what's happened."

"That should make Nicky happy. Then she'd be first with the research on the orphaned bassoonists. You know, it was Roberta who broke into the library first last night and stole two volumes of manuscript music. One of them seems to contain original bassoon music by a relative of the Sandrettis."

"That's one last piece of the puzzle cleared up, then," said Anna, opening the door for me. We went out and started down the stairs. "I thought that Marco forced his way in to make it look like a break-in. Where is Nicky, by the way?"

"Still in bed, I believe," I said. "With Giovanna."

Anna gave me a sidelong look. For a woman who had probably killed in the line of duty, she was surprisingly shy. "You share a house in London, but you're not . . ."

"She's given me an attic room to store my things," I said. "Out of the kindness of her heart."

"I sometimes have business in London."

"I'm sometimes there."

"Perhaps we could . . ."

"Take in a bassoon concert," I said. "Or perhaps an oboe performance, since that's your instrument."

"You wretch," she said, as we reached the lobby and walked by the desk clerk. She threw down the key as she gave me a kiss that surely rocked his unflappability forever. "You know that the trombone is really what I'm good at."

Twenty-two

I TOLD MYSELF that the little paper store was on the way to the Piazzale
Roma, where I'd catch the bus to the airport. I told myself I'd just
walk by. I would just look through the window a second. I didn't
have to go in. I had no reason to go in. Yet as soon as I saw the girl
with the red-gold hair sitting behind the desk, scribbling in a notebook, I couldn't help myself. A CD was playing as I opened the door
and she smiled up at me. The tune was one I would remember her
and Roberta by: *Between the Devil and the Deep Blue Sea.*

"*Buon giorno,*" I said. "I need some ink, I've decided. I want inks
the color of burgundy wine, sepia and indigo. And I want a pen, a
glass pen with a gold nib. I need them all very quickly."

I gathered what I wanted, and Francesca wrapped everything
beautifully, melting a drop of red wax on the knotted string and stamp-
ing it so that it looked like a soft, flattened heart. I didn't tell her I
was leaving. I didn't tell her about Marco's arrest. She said she'd
almost finished her story; she would send it to me when she was
done. She asked me if the inks and pen were a present. I said yes, but

for myself. I didn't tell her good-bye, but I pressed her hand as I left. It was enough for me to see her again, as I had seen her the first time. With Anna de Hoog's touch still all over my body, it seemed strange to want Francesca as my last image of Venice, and yet I did.

I did.

The heart is a strange little instrument. It plays in all registers, up and down the major and the minor scales. Nicola would say that the bassoon captures the complexities of the spirit best, but I put my money on the clarinet, with its knowing wail that restores hope, even in history, and makes adolescents of us all, especially in love.

I settled into my seat on Air Italia. Just before we took off into an autumn twilight glazed with vermilion and warm gray, a last passenger came aboard. He had a long, paper-wrapped parcel that looked strangely familiar. Did he dare? Should I tell a flight attendant Albert Egmont was smuggling out a national treasure? Or should I wait for him to be caught at Heathrow? Would I walk right by him as they took him away? Or would I give Anna de Hoog a call to let her know that business might take her to England sooner than she expected? He caught me watching him as he stowed his package carefully overhead.

With a wink he sat down. A moment later his card, with the Buxton antique shop's address on it, was passed back to me. "Spaghetti," he had written. "The very long kind."

I took out my three remaining books and looked at them. One of them I would have to translate if I were to eat this winter. It could be this one, the story of an older woman falling foolishly in love. Or this one, the story of a strange journey to a distant land. Or perhaps this one, which I had overlooked because its cover was so drab, the story of . . .

I began reading, and as soon as I began, I knew. It was the right book. It was the perfect book.

I could tell already: It was going to become mine.

About the Author

Barbara Wilson's many published works include two other Cassandra Reilly mysteries, *Gaudí Afternoon* and *Trouble in Transylvania*, and a collection of stories, *The Death of a Much-Travelled Woman* (Third Side Press). *Gaudí Afternoon* will be released as a film starring Judy Davis, Lili Taylor and Juliette Lewis in 2001. Wilson's memoir, *Blue Windows* (Picador), was nominated for the PEN West Award for Creative Nonfiction, and won a Lambda Literary Award. She is currently completing a travel narrative about the North Atlantic. She lives in Seattle.

Selected Titles from Seal Press

Gaudí Afternoon by Barbara Wilson. $10.95, 0-931188-89-X. Join globetrotting translator Cassandra Reilly in this high-spirited comic thriller set in Barcelona, home of the celebrated architect Antoni Gaudí. Soon to be a major motion picture starring Judy Davis and Lili Taylor.

Trouble in Transylvania by Barbara Wilson. $9.95, 1-878067-23-0. Cassandra Reilly is on the road again, this time to China by way of Budapest, when a series of chance encounters on a train leads her to the mythic Carpathian mountains of Transylvania.

If You Had a Family by Barbara Wilson. $12.00, 1-878067-82-6. An unforgettable novel about a woman who struggles to come to terms with memories of her childhood and gains a greater understanding of what family is and can be.

Girls, Visions and Everything by Sarah Schulman. $12.95, 1-58005-022-0. Lesbian-at-large Lila Futuransky is looking for adventure on the sizzling streets of New York City, with her keys in her pocket and a copy of *On the Road* in her hand.

Margins by Terri De La Peña. $12.95, 1-58005-039-5. A memorable portrait of the Chicana lesbian as daughter, sister, aunt, friend, writer and lover.

Working Parts by Lucy Jane Bledsoe. $12.00, 1-878067-94-X. An exceptional novel that taps the essence of friendship and the potential unleashed when we face our most intense fears.

Out of Time by Paula Martinac. $12.95, 1-58005-020-4. A delightful and thoughtful novel about lesbian history and the power of memory, set in the antiques world of New York City.

Alma Rose by Edith Forbes. $12.95, 1-59005-011-5. The engaging story of Pat Lloyd and her encounter with Alma Rose, a charming and vivacious trucker who rumbles off the highway and changes Pat's life forever.

The Dyke and the Dybbuk by Ellen Galford. $12.95, 1-58005-012-3. A highly unorthodox tale of one London lesbian and her Jewish ghost. Winner of the Lambda Literary Award for Best Lesbian Humor.

Seal Press publishes many books of fiction and nonfiction by women writers. To order from us directly, call us toll free: 800-754-0271. Visit our website at www.sealpress.com.